AN EYE FOR AN EYE

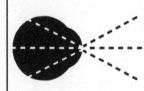

This Large Print Book carries the
Seal of Approval of N.A.V.H.

THE TALES OF ZEBADIAH CREED

AN EYE FOR AN EYE

MARK C. JACKSON

THORNDIKE PRESS
A part of Gale, a Cengage Company

GALE
A Cengage Company

Farmington Hills, Mich • San Francisco • New York • Waterville, Maine
Meriden, Conn • Mason, Ohio • Chicago

Thorndike Press® Large Print Western.
The text of this Large Print edition is unabridged.
Other aspects of the book may vary from the original edition.
Set in 16 pt. Plantin.

LIBRARY OF CONGRESS CIP DATA ON FILE.
CATALOGUING IN PUBLICATION FOR THIS BOOK
IS AVAILABLE FROM THE LIBRARY OF CONGRESS

ISBN-13: 978-1-4328-4654-1 (hardcover)
ISBN-10: 1-4328-4654-X (hardcover)

Published in 2018 by arrangement with Mark C. Jackson

FEB 21 '18

Printed in Mexico
2 3 4 5 6 7 22 21 20 19 18

Dedicated to my mother and
my collaborator,
Judith Ann Jackson

ACKNOWLEDGMENTS

I am so very grateful to my loving wife, Judy Walsh-Jackson, for your patient understanding and loving support for what it has taken to write this book. You inspire me every day of my life.

I am so very grateful to my children, Denise, Joshua, and Sarah, for your patience and love during my four-year obsession with writing and finishing this book.

I am so very thankful to my mother, Judith Ann Jackson. Through our collaboration, you have inspired me to find out who Zeb really is, as you seem to know him better than me. Your voice rings true through my phone with, "Honey, Zebadiah wouldn't ever say a thing like that!" THANKS MOM!

I am so very thankful to my sister, Linda, for sharing my obsession with creating something worthwhile and whole out of nothing but our imaginations.

Thank you to everyone in the San Diego

Professional Writers Group for all your support, especially our fearless leader Chet Cunningham who, at one of our read and critiques, asked me if I had done the research on how long it takes a man to bleed out. If it weren't for you, I would have stopped at five thousand words. You forced me to tell the whole story!

I thank Matt Cunningham for introducing me to your grandfather who "has written like four hundred books and might want to read your story."

I thank my great friend Pamela Haan for your moral support and unknowing guidance in finding the strong, fearless women Zeb meets along the way.

I thank my mountain-man friend Tim Chandler for allowing me to wear buckskins, shoot your black-powder rifles, and to help me feel what it must have been like to live in Zeb's time.

And last but not least, I am grateful to the San Diego Writers Inc. and their Flash Fiction class where I wrote a little story called "The Hanging" and found my good friend Zebadiah Creed.

PREFACE

I have lived my whole life on a whim, and continue to live in this light today. The words I have written down on these pieces of paper reflect my life in such a way that I myself am surprised at the outcomes, good and bad, right and wrong. The end of one story is always the beginning of the next, as it should be, until there are no more stories left to tell. A long and winding path taken through many lands and oceans, often to find oneself circled back to the beginning and, some would say, quite a fitting end.

I have never considered myself a writer, though with the first publishing of my story "The Hanging" in the periodical *The Atlantic,* it would appear to others that I am. I have come late to this profession and only through the strong suggestions and guidance by my gracious friend, Sam Clemens, am I able to resemble a real writer, much less a published one such as himself. He taught me to be fearless in my writing and not back down to those who would censor the words I choose to use. He said to write with confident humility and never give in to those demons all true writers stir up from the dust of the earth and in our own minds. To my friend and fellow writer, I say thank you. I am and will always be grateful for your kindness and support.

The story you are about to read is true, or as much of the truth as I can recollect. To shine a light back to when I was a young man of twenty-five, has been trying and at the same time exhilarating. To write about my brother Jonathan's death and the subsequent repercussions has brought a flood of memories that I thought for years had been left behind somewhere along the great Mississippi River. Though the muddy water disappears to become whitewash behind a steamboat's paddle wheel, it is still muddy water, long after the last trace of the steamboat is gone. I have learned lately not to drown but to float gently down the big Muddy, on to New Orleans, to the end of this story, and the beginning of the next.

Zebadiah Creed
The Continental Hotel
Mendocino, California
October 1880

CHAPTER 1

Lower Missouri River, late summer 1835

Ten or so miles up from Glasgow, a steamer hit our keelboat square, whirled us off her bow, and sent us scraping down the right side toward the single paddlewheel. Jonathan used his guide oar and shoved away from the slow-spinning slats, only to slam us against the wheel's outer rim. We were swamped by churning whitewash but did not break in two. The steamer traveled on downstream, through the early-morning fog and out of sight.

We carried three packs of fifty or sixty beaver pelts each on board and with our boat half-flooded, sat low in the water. In early spring, the Missouri ran fast and deep with snowmelt. It being late summer, we hit a sandbar head on thirty feet from shore.

Jonathan glared back at me. "What the hell, Zeb?"

I operated the rudder.

We bailed out water and rocked the boat side to side, loosening the hull from the sandbar but not free. Stripping naked, I jumped into the chilly river to try to dig us out with a wood plank, almost catching my arm as the boat shifted. I was about to climb back aboard when Jonathan whistled his high, shrill warning.

A square barge, a third larger than our 16-footer, was headed right at us. One man squatted on the bow ready to throw lines. Another held the aft rudder. A third stood at the pilothouse with a foot propped on an over-turned water pail, his arms folded across his chest.

"Lookin' like ya might need a hand or two, or three!"

I pulled myself up onto the platform behind the tiny cabin and reached in the open port for my pistol. Jonathan glanced at me and shook his head, then looked back to the barge drawing close.

"Obliged for the help," he hollered, caught the first rope, and tied it up to the front cleat.

"If ya had a flatboat like ours here, that there bar wouldn'ta snagged ya." The man at the pilothouse yelled back, "You there, naked, with a pistol, we ain't here ta hurt-cha nor steal from ya. An' there ain't no whores 'round ta plug yer pecker in!" The other men snickered. " 'Sides, ya took a mighty turn at the wheel a' that steamer an' I bet yer powder may be a bit soggy?"

I laid down my pistol and slipped on my buckskin britches, smock, and belt, my long knife and tomahawk at the ready. As Jonathan used a hook to retrieve a second rope from the water, I moved forward to cut the first rope if need be.

"Baumgartner's my name . . ." The man took off his top hat and bowed. His hair, what little he had, lay plastered across his forehead. His crooked smile showed almost perfect teeth. He was tall and lanky, skinny even. His clothes were made for style and of fine cloth, but that day had come and gone. He seemed less a man of substance then a man of airs.

As they pulled alongside, the squatter jumped to our running board, nearly knocking me into the water with the long pole he balanced at his chest. He stepped onto one of the wet beaver packs, squished his toes into the soaked deer hide cover, then jumped back to the running board and on up to the bow. The other man stood ready by the barge's rudder.

". . . And if ya please, Rudy there, an' me an' Ole Jeffery here'll pull ya outta this mess ya find yerselves in," Baumgartner declared.

Jonathan tied the second rope around the back cleat. I moved up and stood within arm's length to Rudy. He thrust the pole into the sandbar as Jeffery worked the barge, turning it into the river's current. Baumgartner, using a wide, flat oar, paddled slowly away from us pulling the ropes taught. Our boat jerked sideways then stopped. Rudy lifted his pole up and thrust it back into the water and sand pushing hard, out and away. We moved again, slow and steady, until we broke free.

Both boat and barge caught the current and were swept to the middle of the river. We stood ready, Jonathan at our rudder and me at the bow facing Rudy. He held the pole across his chest, staring at me with a knife in his belt. I turned and looked back as Jonathan pulled his rope bringing the rear of the barge closer. I did the same. Rudy stood motionless with a slight grin on his face, humming a simple tune. As we drew close, Jeffery must have turned the rudder making their square bow swerve toward us. I ran the slack out of my rope as Jonathan raced to draw the rear of our boat even with the barge. Rudy was back up on the running board tipping us sideways. He threw the pole across the water and jumped several feet to land with a grunt beside Baumgartner. I pulled my knife as the ropes went limp, thrown into the river by Jeffery and Rudy. We drifted apart.

"Gentlemen, I say bye, bye fer now. We'll get them ropes back from ya another time!" Baumgartner exclaimed and bowed once more, holding the top hat at his chest. The sun glared off the water and his bare head. He straightened up and smiled, showing his perfect teeth one more time.

To his men he bellowed, "Off we go my fellow Rusty Guts, off we go!"

We were half a mile from the barge when Jonathan asked, "Figure they helped 'cause a' their good hearts?"

Staring back upriver, I did not answer.

"Thought not," Jonathan muttered and continued to steer us away from Baumgartner and his men.

CHAPTER 2

We passed Glasgow at midday; the steamer was berthed next to two barges. Blue smoke belched from both its stacks, as if the captain was anxious to get on with business downriver. Packs of what looked like deerskins, maybe ten or twelve, were being unloaded off one of the barges then loaded and stored onto the steamer's outer decks. Deerskins commanded almost as good a price as beaver. It seemed any animal skin was bought back in the Eastern cities and in France and England.

The American Fur Company owned the steamboat. Of the companies Jonathan and I had traded with, including the Rocky Mountain and Santa Fe Traders, they were the most competitive and ruthless.

A month earlier at Rendezvous, I tried working with their two agents, a man named Fitzpatrick and another named Fontenelle, for a fair sale of our furs. They told me the markets back east were drying up then threatened to undercut our profit by thirty percent. When I suggested we take the furs downriver to St. Louis and find out for ourselves, Fitzpatrick laughed and said we would not make it to the Mississippi without getting taken over, or worse.

I was not to be put on by a scoundrel like him and said as much, calling him a thief. He laughed again and stood up. I hit him in the face, shattering his glasses. As Fontenelle disappeared into the shadows, their men went for me. Stepping back, I pulled both pistols, staving them off. The trappers behind me also pulled their pistols along with knives and tomahawks. As Fitzpatrick wiped shards of glass and blood from his eyebrows and nose, I bid him and Fontenelle good day and left their tent office and compound. I despised being forced into a proposition by intimidation, and being laughed at. Jonathan's reaction to my decision was none too happy once he realized he was to make a thousand-mile trip to St. Louis and back.

There at the pier in Glasgow sat the company steamer, which five hours earlier had almost sank our furs and us. I looked down and rubbed the fresh scars on my knuckles.

We passed anonymously, with nothing said between Jonathan and me.

Baumgartner followed us. Enough behind to appear like any other barge on the river, yet close enough to keep us wondering.

"The other side a Arrow Rock an' past Jameson Island's a creek. We can lose 'em there," Jonathan declared as he navigated the wide bend that wound around the well-known landmark. He worked the boat cross current toward the southern shore and into the afternoon shadow of the bluff. Spying the creek, we slipped our boat easily through its mouth. Jonathan stood on the platform behind the cabin and guided us upstream. I rowed from the middle of the boat, my oars almost touching both banks. Before the first bend, through overhanging trees, we stopped and watched Baumgartner and his crew float past.

"That's that," I said, relieved.

"Reckon so . . ."

About a mile up the creek, we found a good-sized clearing, large enough to off-load our pelts. They were wet and we had to dry and re-pack them before they became damaged goods. Once on the ground, Jonathan cut the willow straps, peeled off the deerskins holding the packs together, and began separating the skins. Most all our possibles were also wet, including flints, percussion caps, and gunpowder. Flints could be wiped down but all I could do with the gunpowder and caps were to let them air dry. It being late afternoon, the sun was not much help. Our three pistols, two Hawken rifles, and the old Kentucky flintlock needed to be oiled as they had already begun to rust. I laid all the powder and guns aside and struck a fire using my flint and steel with a bit of char-cloth. I hung the rest of our belongings — clothes, bags, and other sundry items — near the flames. We had deer jerky and pemmican left from Rendezvous and the flour somehow stayed dry, so there were biscuits to be made, and coffee.

Jonathan separated the pelts, still folded, and laid them out across the clearing. There were a hundred and fifty-three in all, with a tattooed mark on each one.

"These skins ain't as bad as I thought," he said. "Don't think they need stretchin' again. A day 'er two in the sun, repacked an' we'll be on our way."

My brother was the real trapper between us. His word was as good as the pelts lying on the ground. He had more to lose than me for he had a Blackfoot wife and son to get back to when our transaction in St.

Louis was finished. I had no one but him.

The late afternoon lingered into a warm summer evening. Katydids echoed through the Missouri forest — comfortable tunes to keep us company after a long, hard day. Sitting still, the sultry air seeped through my smock and clung to my skin. From somewhere near wafted the faint scent of mint, to be found in the morning for tea. The darker it got the more fireflies appeared out of nowhere to swarm our camp. Fallen stars to guide wandering spirits back to the netherworld, as Jonathan would say.

Our fire was small and we kept our voices hushed, not knowing what or who might be lingering at night in the forest. With no pistols or rifles ready, all we had were our knives and tomahawks in case unwanted guests were to visit. After supper we smoked. Along with the flour and coffee, our tobacco had stayed dry. With little conversation, Jonathan lay down on a bed of leaves, pulled his hat down over his eyes, and in minutes began to snore.

CHAPTER 3

The night was peaceful. Only twice the katydids grew quiet as some creature passed through the forest. Jonathan slept and I kept watch until around midnight. When I woke him, he was speaking our old tongue, asking me to heat the water for redroot tea.

I answered in English, "Brother, I have only coffee. Tomorrow, I'll make us up some mint tea, I promise."

He wiped the sleep out of his eyes and accepted the cup I handed him. Holding it in his left hand, he picked up a piece of dry wood, leaned over, and laid it on the fire. It caught immediately, opening up the circle of light surrounding our camp. Black pelts lay scattered about on the damp ground. Jonathan's face lit up, his eyes did not.

"Where'd you go tonight?" I asked.

"I was with Mother." His voice was low and hoarse, as if something down inside his throat wanted out.

"We was in our tipi, like when we was young-uns. All I remember was the cedar smell of the fire, an' sage, an' taste of buffalo tongue. An' 'course, the freezin' cold outside, how warm it was inside. I was the same age as now but Mother, she was young, like when she would hold me as her new son." He smiled and looked up. "She was singin' softly. Weavin' the blowin' wind an' rain into her evenin' song . . ." Jonathan lowered his eyes again and stared back at the fire. "But to herself. Not for me, as if I weren't even there."

Though I was bone tired and ready for sleep, I sat silent and listened.

"A gust a' wind blew the flap open and there stood a man. More a shadow. Not Father, another man, a white man young as Mother, wearin' a cross shinin' on its own. She was afraid but I wasn't. I felt so I knew him though I can't remember ever meetin' him." Jonathan stopped and laid another stick on the fire. "Like ya see someone where ya never been and a feelin' comes outta nowhere."

He rubbed his eyes again and looked right at me, "And you knew him too."

Jonathan had shared his dreams or visions many times before and I took them in stride. I rarely dreamed and didn't care for being drawn into his. Frankly said, there were times I resented his abilities.

"Mighta been our father," he said, still staring at me.

"What are you saying? Our fathers ain't no white men."

"Father, 'fore we was taken," he answered and turned away.

I stood and looked across the fire to him. We rarely spoke of the time before. For Jonathan, it was less than a distant memory. Ghosts from another past he could not remember, except through his dreams and visions. For me, they were memories I would as soon forgotten.

He stood and in the dark checked a couple of the pelts, caressing then blowing on them. I knew he had finished telling me the story, though it was not the end to his dream, and I did not care to question him further.

He changed the conversation.

"I met them men before, up at Rendezvous. Not that Baumgartner feller, never seen him 'til yesterday. After you hit that company man, the other two came a sniffin' and a scratchin' and offerin' to buy our pelts. Hell, they was still stretched-out plews when they came 'round."

"Did they mention who they represented?"

"No. I figured they was representin' themselves. 'Sides, I told 'em you were the one to talk to."

"Hmm, ain't nobody independent, except you an' me, brother," I smiled.

Jonathan leaned over, picked up another pelt, and carried it back to the fire. "Woulda soon as sold 'em, I'd be with Yellow Bird and our son now."

"And be out the profits we'll make in St. Louis? We been over this and agreed."

"Yes."

"Good, 'nough said. Now about Baumgartner and his men, I don't think they're a harm but we need to stay vigilant, our eyes wide open all the way to St Louis. 'Sides, it's too late to turn back now, ain't it? If they come for us we'll take 'em on like all them others who thought they could take on the Creed brothers!"

Jonathan shook his head while stroking the pelt. He gained the faraway look he so often showed when his mind went elsewhere. I had gathered grass to sleep on and was about to lie down.

"Zeb, I expect to be home 'fore real winter sets in."

"Should be . . ." I muttered, "Should be." I was asleep before my head hit the ground.

24

CHAPTER 4

The morning came early. I held my promise and found the mint a few feet into the forest, rekindled the fire and boiled water. I made biscuits and coffee.

Before the sun was up Jonathan had begun building a press to repack our pelts once they dried. It was primitive, like most trappers of our lot. Not at all like some of the presses used at Rendezvous and other traders' camps. The fanciest was brought up by the American Fur Company and set at Fort William, at the mouth of the Yellowstone River. It had a huge screw with thick, iron plates that pressed the pelts to a width of mere inches. Jonathan built his press out of six posts tied together as a frame. Using a long pole and chain attached to the base of a tree, we were able to pack the furs for transport. With our possibles, powder and caps dried, and our guns well oiled, we were ready to travel on.

The boat was loaded by sunset and turned downstream. We decided to stay there that night then leave before dawn the next morning. Expecting to be at the mouth of the Missouri and onto the Mississippi by late afternoon, I prepared in my mind for the busyness of both rivers. Weighing the dangers and potential success of our endeavor, I was confident of the future.

The katydids were silent that evening. With little conversation between us, Jonathan held the first watch. I lay my head to the ground and went right to sleep.

I heard the click and scrape of a flintlock, the sizzle of a spark, then silence. I opened my eyes to see Jonathan swiftly turn, pull a tomahawk from behind his back, and throw it through smoke into the forest. With the crack of bone and mush, a man fell from the shadows forward to the ground. His skull split through half his face, with the tomahawk still buried. I sat up and pulled my pistols. There sounded a muffled *sha-boom* from the forest directly in front of me; then another, louder *sha-boom* from behind. Blown back against a tree, I felt a piercing sting through my right shoulder, the pistol in that hand violently thrown away by the impact of the shot. Still holding a pistol in my left hand, I reached up and felt a hole. I ran my finger through the torn cloth and touched the burnt skin and blood beginning to flow down my arm.

"I told you bastards no shootin' 'less we have ta!"

Two men crept out of the forest into my view, one tall and lanky and the other short and squat. The tall one stood over the man lying on the ground, then turned him over, "Now, look at poor ole Jeffery. I do believe he ain't dead!"

Jonathan sat slumped over, motionless. Rudy moved around him and added a couple of sticks to the fire, brightening our camp. I could see Jeffery writhing in pain. Baumgartner slid a boot away from his clawing hand.

I took aim and shot. Baumgartner's hat blew off his head and landed in the clearing. Rudy was at my side in an instant with a knife at my throat.

"Don't kill him, don't kill him now! He's spent, can't ya see?" Baumgartner hollered, waving a hand through the air where his hat used to be.

Rudy leaned into my face, real close, and smiled. I smelled his whiskey breath. "You one lucky buck tonight, hear me?" he said and nicked my left cheek by an inch. I swatted the side of his head with my pistol the best I could, knocking him back and away. He was about to run me through the neck when Baumgartner stepped up and grabbed his arm, pulling him off me.

"I said no more killin'!"

I heard a moan. Jonathan lifted his head and looked around, dazed.

"Well, sir, you ain't dead, are ya?" Baumgartner turned away from me, chuckling. "The only one dyin' now's my man who's got a hatchet in his head." With a boot, he shoved Jonathan backward to the ground and kicked away his knife and pistol. Stepping back over to Jeffery, he kneeled down and leaned in close. While whispering to him, he grabbed the handle of the tomahawk and yanked. Dark bits of Jeffery's brain, broken skull-bone, and drying blood came tearing loose, smeared against the glint of the blade. By the fire, I saw his whole body twitch a couple of times then he was still. Using Jeffery's shirt, Baumgartner slowly wiped the tomahawk clean and handed it to Rudy.

"I sell to Frenchy, in St. Louie," he said casually and tucked it into his belt.

Baumgartner, still leaning over Jeffery, whispered a last couple of words then stood up shaking his head. "Now, on to our business," he said and stepped to Jonathan. Rudy joined him. "Let's tie the slogs an' we can talk a bit."

They both picked up Jonathan and threw him against the tree. With a rope from our boat, Rudy tied us together. Jonathan slumped into my right shoulder, sending razor-sharp pains through my chest and arm. Where the ball lie buried deep in my back, I felt nothing but the dull thud of my heartbeat. The forest came alive with the chirping of katydids.

If I'm to dyin' tonight it will be with my brother.

I closed my eyes.

Baumgartner slapped me awake as he did Jonathan.

"No time for sleepin', gents," he said, kneeling in front of us. Rudy had rekindled the fire to a blaze, lighting up an empty camp and our loaded boat moored on the creek. Jeffery had been pulled away with only the blood-soaked ground to show where he died.

Jonathan stirred and opened his eyes. "Take what ya need and leave me an' my brother be." A trickle of blood ran out his mouth.

"I was the one who hit yer man. Didn't figure the Company'd come this far for vengeance," I said with a hoarse voice.

"Comp'ny? Hell, we ain't with those thievin' prigs. Fact is, I respect a man standin' fer his own 'gainst them bastards. It's that we, meanin' me an' Rudy here, poor Jeffery, if he were still livin', an' others not here, have a' interest in them furs you an' yer brother was takin' downriver."

I was bewildered by his speech. "You're sayin' the Fur Company has not sent their agents to steal our furs?"

Rudy spat. "Ain't no goddamn Comp'ny man."

"Rightly so, Rudy, rightly so. Fact is we're comp'ny men of a different sort." Baumgartner gave a slight smile. "We represent a man who don't believe in sharin' the wealth with no middle man, meanin' the man 'tween the beaver an' him."

"The man's name?" I asked.

"Why, a Mr. Benjamin Brody, if ya must know."

"St. Louis?"

"Oh, no, sir, St. Louie's too back-washy fer as big a Brit as Mr. Brody." Baumgartner laughed with almost a sneer on his face. "No, sir, he lives way south, down New Orleans."

"Why you talk so much?"

He turned his sneer to Rudy, looked down

his nose at him, and declared, "By afternoon, these here brothers'll still be tied to this tree an' dead. If it ain't from bleedin' outta the holes we shot through 'em, critters from them woods gonna eat 'em. No matter, we'll be long down the river to St. Louie. So load up, ya Rusty Gut, we're off at first light!"

CHAPTER 5

I heard someone singing.

It was near dawn and I had drifted off. The forest surrounding our fire was black and silent, as if there was no world left beyond the flames Rudy kept feeding. I heard a Lakota death song, barely audible, a whisper under breath. Sung aloud only for the man who was dying. The singing stopped and I felt Jonathan cough. A deep, gurgling, bloody cough that rattled my shoulder he leaned against.

Baumgartner lay on the grass bed with his head propped on his shooting bag. He spun the top hat in his hand by the brim around and around, then stopped and stuck a finger into the hole I shot through. My aim was three inches high from putting a ball through his head. He sat up, turned to me, and smiled, his teeth reflecting the flames of the fire. Still holding the hat, he stood, stepped across the clearing, and put a pistol to my forehead.

"This here hat was a gift from Mr. Brody. Ain't the best I had but a fine beaver hat indeed. An' now it's got a hole shot clean through both sides." Baumgartner cocked the pistol. "Ya ever had a hat like this here hat?"

"No, sir, I ain't."

"I can't hear yer talkin', mister." He pushed my head up against the tree with the pistol's barrel. "Speak up with some spunk in yer words!"

I spat out, "No, sir, I ain't never wore nothin' like it before!"

He placed the top hat onto my head, gently tapping it down. The brim scraped the bark of the tree. He pulled the pistol away and stepped back.

"Ain't this the reason for your killin' all them beavers packed over yonder in yer boat?" He leaned back in and tapped it again, lowering the left side almost to my ear. It smelled of river sweat and piss.

"Don't he look good?"

Rudy glanced up from sharpening Jonathan's tomahawk and mumbled, "Ever' buck should wear one."

Jonathan began singing again, this time louder and stronger. The vibration of his voice resonated through my body. I felt stronger.

"Soundin' like a red nigger," Rudy stood and stretched, still holding the tomahawk. "God, I hate 'em."

"Now, Rudy, them native folk is our friends." Baumgartner smiled again, a quick flash of white on a face covered in shadow.

The hat was still on my head, tilted to the side. Jonathan sang his death song. I looked up into Baumgartner's burning eyes.

"Kill us and be done. Else you're a walkin' dead man, both of ya."

Rudy was beside Baumgartner swinging the tomahawk from one hand to the other. "Day's dawnin', soon them bugs come up an' eat yer skin. Eat holes right through 'til ya ain't no more but bones."

They both stood silent for several seconds.

"One of ya's gonna die this mornin', fer sure. Fer Jeffery's sake."

Baumgartner placed the pistol to Jonathan's head and pulled the trigger.

The concussion blew my right ear out and the hat off my head. I must have fallen over for he grabbed my hair and jerked me back upright. Through the smoke of the shot his face peered into mine, close. He leaned into my left ear and whispered, "Think twice 'fore ya go shootin' holes through 'nother man's hat." Then said casually, "Don't kill him. Knock him in the head once an' make him sleep. Oh, an' get our rope!"

Rudy stepped up, holding my brother's tomahawk in both hands.

"This gonna hurt'cha, buck."

He swung down and the world went black.

CHAPTER 6

I lie on the bottom of the river with my right arm caught underneath the hull of a broken, sunken boat. I reach a hand up, breaking the surface of the water. A rope is laid gently across my palm and I pull it tight. One arm is wrenched up and away toward the glittering sun. The other arm is buried deep, up to my shoulder in the silt and sludge of the black river bottom.

The rope goes slack. I lie beneath the boat holding my breath and the rope.

I tried opening my eyes and could not. They were stuck shut. I raised a hand and heard a dog growl, so close its breath was on me. It backed off a bit and with two fingers I pried my right eye open. The sunlight was excruciating. The dog licked my face and the left side of my head. With every touch of its rough tongue a ratcheting pain surged through my body. I tried knocking it away but could not. The dog kept on licking, barking, and growling, as if it was protecting something. I then realized there were two of them. They had begun to fight over my bloody wounds and Jonathan's dead body.

"I found 'em, Papa," somebody yelled. "I think one's alive!"

I closed my eye. The light and pain began seeping away and I drifted back to sleep.

I hear singing.

A single voice begins. Others chime in, one by one. A choir of voices spiral through me. Call me. I see no light, only a black void, opposite of light yet warm, comfortable.

I feel no pain.

I know no past or future, only the presence of my brother. The choir fades to his single voice, then nothing.

I was out for a long while, maybe as much as two days and nights. I never asked for how long. When I woke, I lay on a straw bed with the smell of an oak fire and biscuits. Something lay with me on the bed. I reached down and felt fur. As I gently stroked the dog, it licked my wrist and arm, comforting me.

I opened my eyes. I saw nothing but moving shadows against muted light. I closed them and touched the side of my head. A dull ache became an intense, shooting pain. I groaned and pulled my hand away from the swollen knot. It seemed the whole top of my head was wrapped in a bandage.

I opened my eyes again. A young woman sat beside the bed. Though I was sweating, I felt cold and began to shake. She laid a cool, wet cloth against my cheeks and forehead, wiping away beads of sweat. My left cheek burned from the cut.

"Shhh now, you're hurt bad. But, we're here and taking good care of you. Make you fit as a Blue Moon in September, Papa likes to say."

For the first time in a year or more, I heard a woman speak in English.

"Your fever's not broke but it's come down some. Papa says the ball went into your shoulder but it ain't come out, that it may have to stay inside you . . ." She took a breath. "That he's seen wounds like this in the war that's healed up fine." She leaned in and wiped my brow. Her buttoned sleeve brushed my cheek. She smelled of lye soap and birch bark. My shaking slowed.

"Papa says you're the lucky one," she whispered and went away.

I fell back to sleep.

I woke to a putrid stink. Rotting meat is what it smelled like, as if someone had left a beaver carcass lying in the sun for two days. I wondered why these folks would allow their cabin to stink as it did.

It was either late afternoon or early morning as sunlight shone dim through the slats in the walls. There was no fire or smells of food cooking, only the dreadful stench of death.

I raised my right arm off the bed a few inches and let it fall back, then squeezed both hands into fists. I was weak but felt I could hold a pistol if need be. My sight was clearer but not quite right.

I wondered where my knife was.

I also wondered where that God-awful smell was coming from.

I could see the silhouette of a man at the foot of the bed. The cabin was dark except for the roaring fire behind him. Steam from a bucket of rocks rose, so intense I could barely breathe. Stripped to the waist with wounds open, I felt sweat and stench pouring from my body, drenching the straw mattress.

"You're still dying."

The man slowly walked around to the

right side of the bed, holding what looked like black mud in both hands. I heard only his whispers and him squishing the concoction together. He spat into the mud and slapped some of it onto my shoulder, slathering the mess deep into the stinking, open wound. Still whispering, almost a prayer, he spat and slapped the rest onto the swollen sore on my head. Before passing out from the heat and pain I again smelled birch bark, and wild onions.

"Now you'll live, young friend, God has said so."

"Biscuits?"

Jonathan slumps at the fire, motionless. I sit across from him, his face lowered into a deep shadow. I cannot see his eyes.

Only his mouth moves.

"Biscuits?"

I see no biscuits on the fire but I smell them and am as hungry as I have ever been in my life.

Around us the forest is light, every leaf shimmers a brilliant green. Katydids sing. White-skin ancestors, ghosts in old, foreign clothes, stand among trees, murmuring words I do not understand. A young man kneels in silence wearing a gold cross around his neck.

"Biscuits?"

Jonathan stands, wearing a war shirt, breach clout, and bear claw necklace. Two black scalps hang loose off a coup ring. They flutter in a slight breeze. At his waist, a tomahawk and knife are tucked into a deerskin wrap. His face is painted red for victory.

He holds a pan out over the fire.

"Biscuits?"

I slowly shake my head.

"Zeb, I do believe it's the first ya ever refused 'em."

My brother smiles, turns, and with fire-flies dancing through the air before him, disappears into the forest.

CHAPTER 7

The morning sun shone through an open doorway, cutting in half the shadow that lay across the bed. I sat up and leaned against the hand-hewn wall of the log cabin. Outside, someone chopped wood and by the sound of the light cut then double split, I knew the young woman swung the axe. Her name was Anna, the daughter of Doctor Joseph Keynes. They were my saviors.

I reached down and stroked the dog beside the bed. A young terrier with some coyote in him, his name was Rascal and he had stayed with me since the day I was found. Two weeks after the bushwhacking my shoulder was healing, with the wound almost closed and less infected. The swelling on my head had lessened and begun scarring though a small cut had been left open to allow for draining. I was given a bottle to ease all my pains but chose to be sparing as not to dull my thinking.

A fire burned low in the fireplace with raccoon stew slow cooking in a Dutch oven. I was not partial to eating raccoon nor did I like the sweet smell but my strength was returning and needed nourishment. I would certainly not turn it away. The day before, the other dog, an old beagle named Juber, had run a mother and one of her young up a tree not too far from the cabin. The doctor shot them down, gutted, skinned, and quartered both raccoons. He scraped the skins clean, stretched them around wood frames, and set them outside to dry in the sun. Though he was maybe in his fifties, he did not struggle. Each movement of his hands was deliberate and exact. Watching him work reminded me of Jonathan and the care he took working our furs.

As I regained my mental sharpness, little had passed between the doctor and me. We had not talked much about what happened, about why I was left for dead. I did not raise the fact that their cabin was certainly within earshot of our camp. Though I was grateful for their kindness, I often wondered why they took so long finding my brother and me.

The chopping stopped and Anna appeared at the door. With her curly, blonde hair tied back, slight freckles showed across her

43

forehead, cheeks, and nose. Tiny beads of sweat moistened her upper lip. Her blue eyes lit up bright when she saw I was awake and she walked on into the cabin. Those last two weeks I had grown extremely fond of her, though I tried not to show it so much. Other than her father, I seemed to be the first man in a while to draw all of her attention.

"You must be hungry, Mr. Creed! I have huckleberry jam and butter with hot biscuits. When you're back from the privy, I'll have you a plate." She smiled and bent to tend the fire. With a white smock belted at her waist, black work pants hung loose on her hips, making her look younger than nineteen. She turned back and smiled again, knowing I would still be watching her.

"Papa's gone to Boonville to do some doctoring, should be back 'fore dark." She paused. "Maybe today's the day to go and see your brother? I know you're still hurting an' all, but I can help you."

She turned away again and I got myself dressed. The smock and deerskin pants I was told had been burned as they were covered in blood. With all my other belongings stolen, I wore traditional long pants and a button-down shirt. Once in fashion back east, they were the doctor's old clothes.

Though they fit well, I did not feel comfortable wearing them.

The privy was around back of the cabin behind a small shed and a corral overgrown with thorn brush. I sat in darkness and wondered if I was ready to see Jonathan. Before, when asked if I wanted to go to his grave, I refused. I had not lost my ability to walk. I had lost my nerve and losing one's nerve was like dying.

Anna came to check on me, as she did every morning. "You still alive in there or you fall down the hole?" She laughed as I answered no. "Well then, your breakfast is getting cold. But you take your time, hear?" Through a narrow gap in the sideboards, I saw her stand very still with her head cocked a bit, as if she was listening for my thoughts. She slowly walked away.

I sat for a long while staring through the boards down the empty path, past the thorn brush and on to the cabin. *I go back to the mountains and no one need ever know the truth of how Jonathan died, keeping my shame buried deep. I head on down the river to find the two bastards and kill them. Maybe, I live out my days on the Lower Missouri with Anna.*

It was a simple decision with lasting consequences.

I finished my duties and strolled back to the cabin, my wounds hurting a little less than the morning before. The hint of cedar smoke drifting through the trees guided me back to Anna. "Reckon I'm ready to go an' see my brother's grave," I announced, walking through the cabin door to sit down for breakfast. She smiled and for once did not say a thing.

Juber ran ahead chasing rabbits and raccoons, real or imagined. Rascal stayed by my side and quiet. Anna talked, her voice dancing ahead of us on the trail. It seemed I was not to get a word in edgewise. No matter, her chatter eased the increasing pain in my shoulder and dizziness from the heat of the midafternoon sun.

We came up a rise to look out over a wide, horseshoe bend of the Missouri River. Cotton clouds sailed through a piercing blue sky, drawing shadows across the land. Several barges and boats, black specks on the water, plied their way up and down the great river. To the north, below Arrow Rock, the creek Jonathan and I traveled up cut through a thin forest connecting the two sides of the horseshoe creating Jameson Island. From where Anna and I stood, the marked trail dropped down a brushy slope and disappeared into the trees. Gazing out across the forest, creek, and trail, I realized how vulnerable we had been, in plain sight to anyone coming and going, by boat or by foot. Jonathan and I were bushwhacked in true fashion and by our own fault.

I followed Anna down the trail with slow, deliberate steps, not wanting to show my weakness. Looking back, she stopped and let me catch her. By noon in late summer, the Missouri forest was hot and sultry and I was sweating like an old mule. I could go no farther and sat down.

Anna kneeled next to me. "You take your sweet time, Zebadiah Creed. Even if night comes along, I can find us a way back. I've grown up in this country and I know every rock and tree and bush, even in the dark." She gave me water from a bladder bag then brushed the hair out of my eyes. "I know it's hard coming here. But you must, for yourself and for your brother's sake." I winced as she laid her hand on my wounded shoulder. "And for the men who did this to you." With her arm around my waist, she helped me to stand and we walked on.

The smell of mint filled the air and the back of my throat became sickly dry. We took a turn off the trail. With the clearing and creek beyond, there stood the dogwood tree where Jonathan and I were tied up. Bloodstains covered the brown bark. At the other end of the clearing, near the cold ashes of our fire, two graves lay side by side.

"Papa used to bring me fishing here," Anna paused, glancing at the banks of the creek and clearing, then over to the graves. "A long time ago."

"Which one's which?"

"Your brother's on the left. When we buried them, we didn't know their names. Still don't know the fellow we found over yonder in the trees. Poor man, you know his face and all. Then the critters must have gotten to him. Or the dogs . . ."

"Jeffery, his name was Jeffery. Jonathan killed him with his tomahawk, after Jeffery's gun misfired." I could hardly talk. Rascal was by my side and with a whimper began nuzzling my shaking hand.

Anna took my other hand. Her long, slender fingers and palm felt dry, cool, comfortable, and strong.

"Did you want to say something, a prayer maybe?"

I closed my eyes and began to sing, softly, under my breath. A song I had not sung for many years, since my mother's death. I thought I had forgotten the words, forgotten the Indian in me, the way of the warrior. I raised both my arms up to the sky and sang aloud.

Letting go of Anna's hand, I began to dance. Rascal barked and raced around me as I slowly circled both graves, picking up fistfuls of dirt and tossing them into the air. Puffs of dust swirled around me, with more dust stirred up by my dancing. Anna stepped back and watched me with a look of wonder. Faster and faster I danced, spinning in tight circles, not so much singing as crying my song, Jonathan's song, of pain and love, death and forgiveness.

I collapsed to the ground in a pouring sweat and lay there for a long while, staring up at the blue sky and passing clouds of the late afternoon. A cool breeze rustled through the branches and leaves of the bloodstained dogwood. Katydids began to sing.

The day will move past into the evening and onto tomorrow. Whether or not I rise from this ground and walk on, these dead men will lay buried here forever.

Rascal gently licked my face. Anna stayed her distance. I rubbed my eyes and blinked away the last of my tears.

Anna spoke, "Oh, heavenly Father, bless

this man and shine new light o'er his pain and loss. Bless his brother and lead him safely to your side in Heaven." She paused and opened her eyes, then closed them quick. "And if you see fit, forgive the men that did these deeds for though they are sinners, they are men with hearts." Through tears, she looked at me with sadness a woman so young should not know.

I could not bring myself to repeat her amen.

CHAPTER 8

Juber busted out of the brush, a gray fox racing ahead of his howls. We were over the rise traveling the trail south, taking our time to leave Arrow Rock in shade and the early dark of the lower forest behind. Rascal ran the fox back into the brush. Juber followed with another howl and would have chased the fox all night had Anna not whistled sharply. Both dogs came to a halt and sat down where they were.

"You handle them well."

"They know they're dogs."

She poured water from the bladder bag into my cupped hands so they could drink. In the waning light, I caught her smile.

Anna and I walked on a ways, up another rise, and stood out in the open facing west. The fiery sun touched distant hills on the horizon and the last hint of day was gone.

"Red skies at night," I murmured.

"Bring a sailor's delight! How do you

know this?"

"Something from my childhood, I suppose."

One by one, the evening stars showed themselves to us. Anna moved close and took my hand. In the deepening twilight, her eyes shone. I felt a stirring I had not felt in a long while, a strong sense of warmth and trust. Something I sensed earlier, as I lay dying. She caressed me with her healing touch and comforted me through the grief from losing my brother.

She eased closer, hesitating, waiting for me.

I let go of her hand. With her arms around my waist, she gently laid her head upon my chest and let out a deep sigh.

I ran my fingers through her curls and kissed the top of her head. Brushing a cheek with my fingertips, I found tears.

"When I first saw you, I thought you dead. We brought you up to the cabin, and you were so bad off. I prayed and prayed that you would live. Then, taking care of you these last weeks and helping you to heal . . ."

We held each other, silent except for our breathing. She noticed me glance up to a glorious sky and broke our embrace.

"No moon tonight." Anna whispered,

"The stars will see us home."

The cabin was dark and the door shut, as we had left it. The raccoon stew still simmered above hot coals. Anna lit two tallow candles and rekindled the fire. With the sweet smell still in the air, I opened the door wide and stepped back out on the porch. The song of the katydids had followed us up from the creek, singing clear and loud.

I fed both dogs dried deer meat and took a piece for myself then fetched fresh water from the well. Exhausted, I sat down at the table and watched her prepare our supper. She looked up from the pot and smiled then laid out three bowls and cups.

"Papa should have been home by now," she said with a frown and ladled her and me stew, keeping her father's bowl empty. "He's done this before you know, leaving me here alone at night while he's ministering."

"I thought he was a doctor."

"He is but he also does a little preaching on the side."

I took a bite of the stew. It was hot and tasted good. "I haven't had raccoon like this."

"Secret's leaving it simmer all day long then scraping the grease off the top and adding onions and rosemary. I learned to cook when we lived in Baltimore, on the Chesapeake. Oh my, I forgot your favorite." She went to the fire, fetched warm biscuits from the morning, and placed them between us.

We ate in silence, with both of us sending glances across the table. When we finished, Anna gathered up my empty bowl and cup in one hand, and with the other stroked my hair and beard.

"Second helping?"

I shook my head. She placed the dishes into the cleaning pot then shooed both dogs outside to the porch and shut the door.

"Your sore head is healing quite nice. How's your shoulder feel?"

I raised my arm and rotated it some. The dull ache where the ball had been removed, I feared, would never go away.

"Healin' up quite nice. Your touch is magic, my dear Anna."

With a deep blush, she smiled. "I'll get Papa's dogwood salve." She went to a shelf covered with various jars and pulled one from the back. "This is from the tree we saw today, by the creek, the only one of its kind for miles. The bark stimulates your skin to leave less of a scar. Now, Mr. Creed, if you will please remove your shirt?"

Anna set the jar on the table, sat down, and pushed a chair up to face me. I hesitated. She reached over and unbuttoned the top button.

"This is no time to be modest." She continued unbuttoning until the shirt hung open.

"Your Papa's been awful good to me, no?"

"Zebadiah, I am the daughter of a doctor and am obliged to help you heal same as him. He doesn't need to be here for this. Besides, him being this late, he won't be back 'til morning."

She stood and from behind, placed her arms around my neck and reached down. I leaned forward. She slowly removed my shirt, her fingertips barely caressing the skin of my chest and back.

"I will wash this tomorrow, along with those pants." She paused and looked me up and down. "And you're getting a bath!"

Though I was given one a few days after my arrival, it seemed I had not bathed in months.

I sat still as Anna touched a finger to the dark concoction and dabbed it onto my shoulder wound. My skin tingled then began to burn. I smelled the tree I had been tied to. It felt as if my bare skin lay against its rough, bloodstained bark. Then warmth began to spread, from my shoulder down through my arm. She leaned in and gently dabbed my left cheek.

"Why the cut on your face? It's as if he marked you for some reason."

"Don't know. But when we meet again, I'll do the same to him."

"Shhh, Zebadiah, no talk of that now. You are safe with me." She dabbed the side of my head, her hand shaking ever so slightly. Soon my face and even my hair burned.

Anna laughed and wiped her hands on a towel and with another wiped the wounds clean of salve. "Earlier you could not handle this. Now this will heal you. It's too late for the other scars on your chest I'm afraid, someday you must tell me of them."

I placed my hand on her cheek and kissed her forehead.

"Someday . . ."

I felt in her a longing, through to her innocent soul. Truth bared naked. I closed my eyes and we kissed.

Deep, we kissed. With a brush of her breast against my hand and the touch of our knees slipped up between each other's legs, I leaned into Anna with a passion. She trembled and pulled away to catch her breath. Flush with excitement, she looked down at my britches and smiled. I drew her in and we stood, holding each other, pressed close; feeling our bodies as a man and a woman. We kissed again, long and hard.

I stopped and tried to back away. She frowned and moved closer, caressing my old scars, tracing them with her fingers. I brushed curls from her shadowed face. She stared up at me as if she were dreaming. We held each other for a long while, until the fire burned down and the flames of the tallow candles flickered low. Not one word was spoken and not one tear was shed.

Anna slowly undressed and eased into her sleeping gown as she did every evening, this time making sure I saw her bare breasts, the flatness of her stomach. Without looking my way, she climbed into her bed.

I let the dogs back in, undressed, and climbed into my bed.

As we lay in the dark, with only the coals of the fire glowing and our breathing heard, she whispered from across the room, " 'Night, Zebadiah Creed."

" 'Night to you, Anna, goodnight, my dear."

"Zebadiah?"

"Hmmm?"

"Come lie with me?" Her breathing stopped.

I stared up into shadowed crossbeams that

held the cabin together. Rascal lay asleep at my feet.

"It ain't right yet."

Anna sighed, as if relieved. Soon her breathing was shallow and steady.

Twice I stood beside her bed watching her sleep, wanting desperately to touch her, to lie with her, and did nothing.

I knew to break the dam was to flood her heart.

I did not want to drown.

CHAPTER 9

Contrary to the sailors' proverb professed and agreed upon the night before, the morning brought rain. The privy's seat was wet and drops fell through the roof, drizzling my head and shoulders. Instead of feeling a deep satisfaction with the last evening's affair, I sat with lingering doubt and confusion. I finished my morning constitutional and with Rascal slowly walked back to the cabin.

Anna stood with her arms crossed, on the porch by the door. Rather than pants and smock, she wore a plain blue gingham dress; her blonde hair hung loose, brushing her shoulders.

I smiled and said, "You didn't come check on me."

"I knew you didn't need help."

I could not tell if she smiled back.

She followed me in and we sat down for breakfast. I nervously rubbed my fingers over the smooth, dark wood of the oak table then reached across for one of her hands. She pulled both away and placed them in her lap. "Papa will be home soon. When he's away all night to Boonville or Arrow Rock, he returns by midmorning."

I finished the stew and used a biscuit to wipe the bowl.

"You look mighty pretty in that dress."

She did not respond and continued to stare out the door. I could not stand the silence between us.

"I thank you for helpin' me yesterday, with my brother . . ."

Anna gave me a slight smile. "I'm obliged to help, Mr. Creed. Do you feel better about your plight?"

"My plight . . ." I paused, thinking how to answer. "I lost all I've owned and loved." I paused again and looked her in the eyes. "But I suppose I'm feelin' gratitude for bein' alive. Now, I'll ask you the same question. How do you feel?"

Her smile disappeared. "I won't presume what matter you ask about, Mr. Creed."

"Last night?"

She cleared the table, dropping the bowls and spoons into the wash pot with a splash. The last of the stew still simmered in the Dutch oven. She leaned over and stirred it with slow, deliberate strokes. With her back to me, she straightened up and stood motionless, holding the dripping spoon. The sudden sizzle of liquid hitting red, hot coals startled her awake.

"I'm no whore."

"Of course you ain't." I exclaimed, maybe a little too quick and loud. "Nor have I thought of you as one." I pushed away from the table and stood up.

Anna turned and was in tears. "When you took me in your arms, I felt overwhelmed and, and well, flushed and, and then we kissed and . . ."

I reached for her hand and she allowed me to draw her in again. She wiped her cheeks and tried pushing me away. I held her tight until she melted in my arms. The rough cloth of her dress rippled as I caressed her back and shoulders. My fingers touched her bare neck and she quivered, then pushed hard against my chest and began beating me.

I let her go and stood alone in the middle of the floor. "Last night, I chose restraint. I felt your passion, our passion an' something happened. I so wanted to join you in your bed but, I could not on account a' my respect for you and your papa."

She cried, as if in anguish, sending both

dogs to barking. I took a step toward her and Juber snapped at me. Then Rascal growled and snapped at him.

"Now look at what I've done, I've called the dogs to fighting!" She sat down at the table then turned her chair away with elbows on her knees and head in hands, gently sobbing. I chased Juber onto the porch with a broom and shut the door. Again, I sat across from her. She sat up straight, rubbed the wrinkles from her dress, and pulled the chair back to the table.

Anna slowly reached across and touched the tips of her fingers to mine. She was flush in the face and smiling. I was flush somewhere else.

She jerked her hand away as footsteps sounded on the porch. The door swung open and Juber bound into the cabin, shaking himself nearly dry. Right behind strode Doctor Keynes.

"Must the dog stay alone in the rain?"

Anna jumped up and threw her arms around her father.

"Oh Papa, you're home and safe!"

"Well, of course, dear, did you expect me not to be?" he said and held her back. "Careful, your dress will get soaked."

He paused and looked at Anna up and down, then glanced past her shoulder to me.

"Mr. Creed, you are feeling much better I see."

"Yes . . . Yes, sir."

There was an awkward silence as the doctor leaned his walking stick into the corner near the door and peeled his pack off his back. He let out a deep, exhausted sigh then a cough. His age shone on his haggard face and slumped shoulders.

"Is there no more stew, my dear? I am famished. I shall eat and rest and then we must discuss a number of issues that relate to you, Mr. Creed, you and your brother."

Anna and I still stood motionless. As he turned his back to us, she glanced at me, letting out her own silent sigh. As Dr. Keynes sat down at the table, she dished out the last bowl of the stew. Within seconds, his chin touched his chest and he was sleep.

I stepped outside onto the porch for fresh air as the sickly sweet smell of the stew collided with whiffs of beer breath. The first crack of thunder must have startled the doctor awake. The door stood partially open. I listened for a while to the quiet murmuring between Anna and her father, then silence except for the rain.

The doctor cleared his throat. "Mr. Creed, would you care to join us in conversation?"

I stretched, breathing in the damp air. A couple of breaks in the clouds allowed streaks of sunlight to shine through the elm trees in front of the cabin. I looked around for a rainbow and there was none. Another clap of thunder sounded farther off in the distance. With the scrape of chairs against the wooden floor, Dr. Keynes and Anna turned to face me as I walked back through the door, into shadow, and sat down.

"You are healing quite nicely," he said.

"Yes, sir. And I thank you, sir, for what you have done, savin' my life." I glanced at Anna. "And of course, your daughter helping . . ."

For a short while, there was silence between us, as if the doctor was collecting his thoughts.

"You and your brother have not been the only victims on the river."

"Sir?"

"I've been told of, as you say, a bushwhacking east of here, downriver past Boonville, not but a day after your tragedy. Over four hundred pelts were stolen and another, the day after, closer to the Mississippi. That take was almost six hundred pelts." The doctor removed his glasses and wiped them clean with his smock. I sensed him choosing his words carefully. "Seems like an ambitious lot to me, and well organized."

"My brother," I said, "left two of three standin' before he was finished off. There can't be that many pelts stolen by them two. If there were more pirates, they didn't show their faces."

The doctor continued, "Well, the word I received was that there may be some roguishness going on within the American Fur Company itself, though this talk was certainly spoken behind the cloak of secrecy." He turned away and took a drink from his cup. I could still smell beer on his breath, which led me to wondering where he had done his ministering the night before. The information he was lending me sounded like tavern gossip.

I stood and went to the door. The rain seemed to have lessened. Though after only a lull it fell even harder, making the sky above the trees seem dirty, like riverbed gravel seen from the side of a keelboat.

Without turning around, I said, "The Company holds most of the fur business, least west a' here through the Rockies north to the Columbia. There's no rhyme or reason to think they would steal from themselves." I took a breath. "How many men did you say were in this gang of thieves?"

I could hear the doctor rustle in his chair, hesitating. "Four or five, I suppose, maybe more. Certainly more than one man can take on." He paused again. "Surely they're on to St. Louis by now."

Standing with my back to both of them I wondered why he offered this information, which may or may not have been true. "The night of our bushwhackin' the thieves mentioned an Englishman, said he lives in New Orleans. Even gave up his name as a Mr. Benjamin Brody; claimed he was the ringleader of the gang, though the murderer Baumgartner seemed to share this information with some bitter resentment." I swallowed. "Sir, the one that hit me with a tomahawk and the other who killed my brother indeed may be in St. Louis but not for long, they are headin' to New Orleans 'fore winter sets in."

I felt Anna's stare upon me. I did not turn around.

"That is where I must go."

"But, but . . ." Anna began then cut herself off, as if she knew not what to say.

"Mr. Creed," the doctor said quietly, "we thought you might like to stay here with us for a while longer."

The scrape of a sliding chair broke the silence. I swung around to face Anna standing not two feet away from me.

"Hear my words, Zebadiah Creed, you are not going anywhere! Why, you could hardly walk to your brother's grave without my helping hand and arm around your waist. And, and besides, you have no weapons to defend yourself. Papa took them all away."

"My weapons?" I gasped. "I thought the thieves stole them along with everything else I own."

Dr. Keynes stood and placed his hands on his daughter's shoulders and gently moved her aside. Though slightly shorter than me, it seemed we stood eye to eye.

"Sir, we found only a knife and pistol in the brush. There was nothing left near you, I'm afraid."

"I am now mighty confused, sir, as to why you haven't told me this before now. Those would be my brother's knife an' pistol, where are they now?" I glared at the doctor then shot a glance to Anna as she stood by the fire.

"Mr. Creed, we are a family of peacemakers. We do not impel violence unless absolutely necessary." He paused again, not drawing his stare from me. "We sir, are very proud Quakers."

"Quakers?" I cried.

"Yes, Mr. Creed."

I stared back at him, unable to turn away. As soon as he said that word, *Quaker,* my gut tightened more and it seemed a hand reached up to clutch my throat.

"I have but one question for you, sir." I choked out, "Did you hear the first shots the evening before that bastard murdered my brother?"

"Yes."

"And you did nothing . . . ."

"We pray for whoever is fighting," he said with quiet conviction. "And save every life we can."

"My mother and father were Quakers."

His eyes lit up. "Then you must be Quaker also!"

"No! My folks were missionaries, an' because a' not defending themselves or their children, they died at the hands of the Lakota, leaving Jonathan and I to become slaves."

"Yet, you rose above your own fate to become a warrior."

"How do you know this?"

"The scars on your chest tell the tale."

"And what tale is that?" We stood toe-to-toe.

"I heard it called Sun Dance from a fellow Quaker who's served in the north. He tells of men hung from thongs tied to pieces of antler pierced through their skin, like meat on a stick. For three days and nights you must've hung."

"Wiwanyang Wacipi . . ." I whispered under my breath. Then, "You've known this the whole time."

"Yes, I suspected as much the day I pulled the ball from your shoulder. Today you have confirmed my suspicions."

I rubbed my shoulder where there used to lie a musket ball, feeling the beginning of a new scar. Anna still stood silent near the fire.

"Dr. Keynes, I have one more question . . ." I lowered my arm and squared back up. "Why have you given me this information, 'bout the robberies?"

"As I said, we wish for you to stay here, with us. Nothing more . . ." He paused and looked down at my clothes, his clothes and boots, then to Anna and back to me. ". . . That if you knew the full rumors of conspiracy, to include far more than the two thieves you faced, you might think twice before seeking your revenge against these men."

"An' what did I give you before now to think I was on my way to find the two?"

"Mr. Creed," he sighed, "I've known men like you, ones who cannot let God do the sorting and the punishing. They feel compelled to sneak around the lord and take lives into their own hand." Again, he looked me in the eyes. "If your brother killed a man and then was killed, the sin has been served. There is nothing by your hand that can be done to change this fact."

"Sir, I don't sneak around nobody, especially a god I left behind years ago, buried on the north plains."

He raised his hand in defense. "Mr. Creed, I mean nothing by this other than to say . . ." The doctor cleared his throat. Then, for the first time of me being there, he coughed deep from his chest; a cough with which I was familiar. He whispered, "Courage is shown through many different acts." He coughed again and sat back down in the chair. Anna went to his side as he bent over, elbows to his knees. She stroked his hair and looked to be in tears. The coughing fit subsided and he slowly sat up straight. "Sometimes, my young friend, the most courageous of men do nothing at all."

I could not listen anymore. No matter what Dr. Keynes said to try to persuade me, my mind was made. I did not believe in destiny, I knew what I was to do.

"I will be leavin' tomorrow," I announced and turned to walk out the door. Anna remained standing at the table, beside her father.

Rascal followed me onto the porch and into the early-afternoon rain.

CHAPTER 10

I wanted my buckskins. The doctor's shirt and pants had dried small from the sun and I was miserable. Rascal seemed to love the summer rain. As soon as it stopped, he shook himself and at the open rise overlooking the Missouri, where Anna and I stood only the night before, lay down on the trail to sun dry.

I did not look west, back toward Arrow Rock and my brother's grave, but to the east toward Boonville and on to St. Louis. The Mississippi was only a few bends away. I had traveled the river once by barge with Jonathan, to Memphis on down to New Orleans. Now alone and with no weapons or money, I did not know how to get there.

The Missouri seemed deserted, except for one lone steamboat paddling downstream with black smoke trailing behind. Boonville would be her next stop. With the shadow of Arrow Rock behind me, I whistled for Rascal and we strolled back to the cabin one last time.

I stumbled seeing my brother's pistol and knife lying on the table. Laid alongside them were my buckskin smock, pants, and moccasins with the blood removed. Burnt sage replaced the sickly sweet smell of the raccoon stew. For an instant, I closed my eyes and could well have been standing in my Lakota father's teepee.

Anna looked up from a shirt she was mending. "The sage was Papa's idea. He thought we'd send you off with the right mind."

Almost unable to speak, I whispered, "And Jonathan's knife an' pistol?"

"Mine. There's a full shooting bag with plenty of powder and balls around somewhere. You can take it when you go, though I still have to find it."

"My clothes?" I rubbed the soft material and fringe gently between my fingers.

"I cleaned them the first week you were here with the local salt from across the river. Makes for a good abrasive."

"Where's Dr. Keynes?"

Wearing the same black pants and smock from the day before, she rose and pulled a pan off the fire grate. "Checking his rabbit snares, I hope. He should be home soon enough with one or two for supper. He didn't say. For now, though, would you like a biscuit?"

I stared into her blue eyes wanting so badly to reach out, to draw her in. She stayed her distance and held the pan out.

I took a biscuit.

She turned her back on me without a word.

Anna chopped wood as I sat on the porch step cleaning both the knife and pistol. The shooting bag was well equipped and with a few drops from a vial of whale oil, I wiped down my brother's knife. With his handle made of elk antler rather than deer, the weight and balance were slightly different than mine. It still felt good in my hand. Anna caught me holding the knife up to gleam in the late-afternoon sun.

"Have you ever killed anyone?"

She shocked me by the question though I did not show it. Most men I knew had killed, at least once and for a variety of reasons. Most men did not discuss the subject with a lady.

"I'm sorry, is that too personal a question to ask a man who holds a knife up to the sun and smiles, like he's holding part of himself?" She laid the axe against the stack of wood and stood with her arms crossed. "Well, have you?"

"Have what?"

"Killed another man?"

"Yes . . ."

"More than one? How many?" she asked, as if I would tell her twenty or thirty.

"Three for sure. Maybe four, I don't know if he died. I couldn't count his coup."

"Count his coup?"

"Take his scalp."

Her face turned pale. I slid Jonathan's knife into its sheath and set it down on the porch.

"Do you . . . do you have their hair?"

"No, they were stolen along with everything else I owned." I frowned. "I hope one day to have them returned."

"To the families of the men you killed?"

"No, no, to me, I'm the rightful owner. I killed 'em!"

She gave me the least bit of a smile. "Show me."

"Show you what?"

"Show me how you take another man's scalp. I may need to know this someday."

I sat for a second staring at her. She turned away toward the trail and the overgrown corral and privy. In the instant it took to reach her, I pulled the knife from its sheath, grabbed a handful of her hair, and threw her down next to the woodpile. With one knee pinned between her neck and shoulder, she struggled to no avail. I slowly drew an outline with the tip of the knife, a circle on the top of her head, and then yanked.

"And with a sucking sound, the scalp pops off," I whispered.

After gently letting go, I offered to help her up. She refused me and lay there for a long while, her chest heaving as she tried catching her breath. With eyes squeezed tight, tears rolled into her dirty, blonde hair. I sat cross-legged next to her in calm silence with my brother's knife sheathed and tucked into my belt.

"Jonathan was more Indian than me. He could scalp a man in one clean cut and leave him alive."

Anna's breathing slowed. Still with her eyes closed, she stopped crying.

"He favored catchin' beaver with a net, beating 'em in the head rather than using a trap. He rode only Indian ponies and could throw a tomahawk fifteen paces blindfolded an' split the two-inch branch of an oak tree. Not once did I know him to sleep in a bed. And never did I see him drunk."

Tears rolled down my cheeks. I sat up straighter.

"If a man showed respect and candor, that man gained his respect in return. But, if someone crossed him there was hell to pay, usually with a pistol or knife bein' pulled. Younger than me when we were taken, he had no recollection of being white an' later had to relearn English. His Lakota mother and father were not my mother and father yet we were raised brothers." I wiped away any remaining tears. "Jonathan's death has come before mine, leavin' a Blackfoot squaw widowed with a young half-breed son."

Brushing sadness aside to taste bitter anger, I defiantly placed a hand on the knife at my belt. "I will always feel responsible."

Rascal came and licked Anna's face until she opened her eyes to stare into the waning, afternoon sky. What few clouds left from the morning's rain glowed pink and orange. She rolled onto her side to face me, propping her head up with one hand.

"Thank you. I now know how frightening it must be to die by yours, or your brother's, knife." She paused to take a deep, calming breath. "Know this, Zebadiah, there is one person in the whole world that is no longer afraid of you."

Still refusing my help, we both stood. She placed her arms around my waist and loosely held me, then leaned up and kissed my neck. She let go and patted my chest twice, smiled, and picked up the axe. "I hear Juber off in the distance but not too far and Papa's got supper. I can always tell by that dog's bark." With the flick of a wrist, she swung the axe into the chopping stump and headed for the cabin door. Over her shoulder she said, "Mr. Creed, you have a mighty journey ahead, you'd best be ready."

The afternoon seeped into evening. Dr. Keynes returned with two healthy rabbits and with three cuts each, pulled the skins off with ease. Saving the innards for gravy, Anna skewered the fresh meat onto a crude rotisserie and laid it over the fire. Soon the smell of sizzling fat filled the cabin, wiping away any trace of sage.

Before supper, the doctor had another coughing fit. Though not as severe as the morning, it seemed each retching of his body wrung a bit of life from him. Anna gave her father comfort by gently rubbing his neck and back. Her glance to me was one of determination and sadness.

The doctor's supper prayer was simple. "Bless this bountiful earth and loved ones, and to cast no stone upon a sinner unless one is sinless." I did not repeat their amen.

We ate in silence.

After supper, I inspected my worth. Jonathan's knife and pistol were ready as was the doctor's shooting bag, though I wished I had a Kentucky long rifle or Hawken. The buckskin felt good in my hands. Anna had stitched up the burnt shot hole in the smock, leaving little to show of any wound. I rotated my shoulder with ease then pulled off my shirt and let Anna dab on the dogwood concoction, this time in full view of her father. My skin burned a little less. She did not touch the other scars.

"I have a favor to ask of you," I said as she put the medicine away. "Would you cut off my hair and beard?"

"Off?"

"Yes."

"We have my razor in the trunk under the bed and scissors in the cupboard," the doctor said. "Mr. Creed, are you looking to disguise yourself?"

"No, sir, tired of lookin' like where I came from. An' if you would, lend me these clothes of yours I'm wearing for a while longer? I would be obliged . . ."

They stared at me then each other.

"Is it your aim to become a sophisticate?"

He gave me a slight smile. "A world weary one at that."

"If I'm going to the city, I want to fit in. Without bein' too much noticed for who I really am."

Anna was ready to say something then stopped.

"Please, Anna," the doctor said. "Speak your mind."

"Well, it seems wherever you go there you are as genuine as ever." She looked straight into my eyes. "You can't hide yourself, Zebadiah, no matter how hard you try."

Dr. Keynes smiled at his daughter. I looked down at the clothes I wore and said nothing.

They both saw me off the next morning, with the doctor giving me three gold eagles worth ten dollars each. Anna gave me a bundle of biscuits and most of the cooked rabbit. She reached up to the medicine shelf and pulled down the dogwood salve. She slipped the jar into my bundle, patted me on the chest, and with a kiss on the cheek said, "For your scars, Zebadiah Creed."

CHAPTER 11

St. Louis, September 1835

The shore and water before us seemed on
fire. Oil torches flickered pale yellow light
upon goods and cargo strewn up and down
the six-mile landing. Shadowed by Blood
Island across the shallow channel to the
east, hundreds of boat lanterns swayed to
the rhythm and flow of the black water's
current. Broadhorn barges, keelboats of all
lengths, timber rafts from the North woods,
and at least thirty side and stern wheel
steamboats glittering white and gold lay
moored three deep along the St. Louis river-
front.

Billy Frieze and I sat out on the forward
veranda, upper deck of the steamboat *Diana*
watching our approach. Drinking Kentucky
whiskey, we wagered whether the captain
and pilot were to run us aground as we
rounded the southern end of Duncan Island
or ram us straight into the river flotilla

before us. By the speed of our approach, either would be disastrous.

"Mate, the captain's been pushin' steam since Columbia, either blowin' the boilers or run into all them boats 'fore we step back onto blessed dry land," Billy said loudly enough for the crewmen manning the pilothouse to hear. Knowing him all of two days and nights, I wondered why I had befriended such a drunk and obnoxious Brit.

I smelled cigar smoke. Fontenelle, the American Fur company's representative, stepped forward from the shadows of an open cabin door to stand behind us. "Ah, St. Louis . . . A sight beholden to New Orleans and all of the beloved cities back east and in Europe. A will and testament to the great riches traded up and down the Mighty Mississippi; the Father of all Rivers." He took a draw then blew smoke between us. "Do you agree, Mr. Creed?"

Without a glance back to him, I said, "Sir, my one-time visit was a day an' a night berthed on a steamer. Can't say much for the city. Though what I saw of the landing, I wasn't impressed." I took a drink of my whiskey. "And now with your captain's rather hasty approach, I may see more of the landing than I care to."

"Ah, ye of little faith." Fontenelle blew

smoke directly at my head. "Our captain is the best, paid very well. So gentlemen, I suggest you relax, sip your whiskey, and enjoy our landing. We shall be disembarking within the hour." He turned and strolled aft and out of sight. I sensed he did not care for my answer.

Owned and operated by the Fur Company, *Diana* carried the last of the beaver packs from the rendezvous Jonathan and I had attended. The first half of the skins was moved downriver by the steamboat that swamped us. One of only nine passengers, I paid seven dollars to travel first class from Boonville to St. Louis. As far as everyone on board was concerned, I was the son-in-law of a business owner from Chicago. Trusting no one, I kept to myself. Only for dining did I join the passengers.

The second evening after leaving Boonville, at dinner, Fontenelle told a story of how he fought off a renegade fur trapper up at Rendezvous and then fought twenty more. "Son-of-a-bitch thought he'd take his furs elsewhere, downriver," he said to no one in particular. "Him and the others, we give a fair price for each pelt. 'Course being the only company up there . . ." Fontenelle smiled and took a drink of his wine, "a fair price is all they got, if you understand my meaning." Then he exclaimed boldly, "God-damn trapper is still shitting beaver pelts out his ass."

Everyone at the table laughed except for me. I rose slowly from my chair and stood frozen until all were quiet. In silence, I bowed graciously to Fontenelle, not taking my eyes off him, then turned and bowed once more showing him my backside.

"Sir, do you not care for my sense of humor?" he asked.

I turned back. "As a businessman with little knowledge of the fur trade, I don't reckon I can say what's fair an' what's not in a sale. Nor do I find secondhand tales humorous." I paused for his reaction. When there was none, I continued. "I do know that for any business, no one profits from stolen goods. An' if rumors are true, sir, the profits lost on eight hundred odd furs are quite a sum for the trapper as well as trader." I turned away and from over my shoulder said, "A loss for everyone except for the thief and his fence." Before he spoke another word, I was up the stairs to my cabin.

Later, a knock came at my cabin door. A man of maybe thirty in mustache and top hat tried pushing his way into the room, only to find a knife at his chest.

"Mate, if you cut me I swear I will bleed like a bloody stuck pig," he whispered in a Brit's accent and, with a finger, gently pushed the tip of the knife away. Trusting he was either unarmed or at least not showing a weapon, I eased down to the bunk, laying my knife beside me. The cabin was tiny but it had a single chair and desk. I nodded for him to have a seat. We stared at each other for a short while without a word spoken. As he had come to me, I was not starting the conversation. He pulled a pint from his jacket and offered me a drink.

"Fontenelle's pissed. You blew out his lantern in front a' them prigs hanging on every word. An' you broke his spell."

I took a drink and let him talk, holding the bottle in my left hand while my right hand still lay on the knife. If the man were to lunge at me, he would soon be dead.

"Been on this steamer since Glasgow, shithole if you're asking. Besides that, I've heard the tale, as you call it, twice now. This time changed from ten to twenty trappers an' him alone fighting them off. Now I'm wonderin', which version of the tale is true." He paused and glanced down. "Might good whiskey, eh, mate."

I took another, longer drink and handed

85

him back the nearly empty bottle. He drank the last of the whiskey down. "What line of business did you say you were in?"

"I didn't," I said, still staring at him.

"I hear you're from Chicago?"

"From who?"

"Fontenelle."

I lowered my gaze. My lying was never very convincing, especially with clean-shaven cheeks.

"So, you an' him are more than dinner acquaintances, then?"

"Oh, no, sir. Your name come up during a card game I attended last night. Is where I won this fine whiskey you been drinking. Oh, no, mate, Fontenelle asked the question, to no one in particular, as to why a man from Chicago in the textile business has no cloth to sell."

I gripped the knife, turning my knuckles white.

The young man glanced down, then leaned in and smiled. "What I said was, ain't nobody's business but his own."

"An' why is a Brit so quick to defend somebody he don't even know?"

He laughed and pulled another bottle from his coat. "By what I've heard an' now seen by your answer to Fontenelle, let's say, we might have sights on the same reputedly

86

stolen furs."

"And how do you reckon I have anything to do with goddamn furs, mister . . . What did you say your name was?" I did my best not to show him my shock; though later I thought that my reaction of defensiveness was what he intended to rise in me.

"Oh how un-gentleman like of me." He stuck out his right hand. "Billy sir, Billy Frieze. I hail from Manchester, England, the hat-making capital of all Europe!"

I did not shake his hand. "You come all this way to find stolen furs, Mr. Frieze? Would they be your stolen furs?"

"No, sir, your stolen furs."

As if I knew what he was to say before saying it, my knife was at his throat. This time he did not push the blade away. He leaned into the tip just enough to dimple his skin. "Truth is, mate, suspicions are already in the minds of those who may or may not have answers to your questions. Kill me now and your future is a dire one. We keep this conversation going and me breathing, you may come to the truth without another ball shot into you." He smiled and winked. "Mate, I may be the only friend you got on the whole Mississippi. Certainly the only one you'll have when you go a stumbling 'round St.

Louis . . . or New Orleans, looking for those two killers."

"Quit talkin'!" I shouted.

Billy licked his lips and backed away from the knife. He raised the bottle of whiskey and offered me a drink.

I felt my chest might explode. The wound in my shoulder had not quite healed, causing my hand to shake. My mind reeled as to what the truth might be, coming from a half-drunk Brit.

"What do you know of my plight?" I willed the knife steady.

"I know about the hole in your shoulder. And I know about your brother."

"How?" I pressed the tip of the blade back into his neck.

"An evening of games and drink."

"Where?"

"Boonville, night or two 'fore we boarded this here steamboat."

I slowly lay my brother's knife back on the bunk and looked down at the doctor's clothes I wore. Billy breathed a sigh. It appeared my charade was over. "Did you meet two men? One tall an' damn near bald, the other one's short."

"I did not. I sat with an old man, a doctor he said he was. An' you ask me, not much of one. Did more bloody preaching then

88

doctoring. Not much of a preacher either, did more drinking then preaching."

I could not respond and sat with my right hand still touching the handle of the knife, the other clasping the open flap of my coat to stifle the shakes. Certainly, Dr. Keynes had not meant to give me up. But for the drink, would he tell my tale to a stranger knowing the cost of a life?

"I know of the two men the doctor spoke of . . . as you speak of them now."

"You know them?"

Billy smiled and glanced away. "I said, I know *of* them."

We sat awhile in silence drinking the last of the second bottle, Billy drinking most.

"You say you sat with Dr. Keynes no more than a week ago yet you traveled downstream on this very steamer from Glasgow. She didn't dock in Boonville 'til after the doctor spent time there." I raised the knife again. "Which is it, mister?"

His eyes glassed up as he swigged the last drink. "Could it be I spent a week 'er two in Boonville rather than Glasgow?" He slurred. "These bloody steamboats all appear the same, you know." Pausing, his eyes cleared. "You are that man . . ."

"Sir?"

"At Rendezvous, you are the trapper Fontenelle mocked."

I did not answer and lowered the knife to my side one last time. He soon departed, stumbling down the hallway toward his cabin. He left me wondering what to make of our conversation, and feeling utterly alone. I certainly did not trust my new acquaintance.

It was then I decided to befriend him, with the hope that his companionship would be the means to a very bitter end.

From the pilothouse one deck above us, a bell rang and the rumbling from deep within the bowels of the steamer began to lessen. As we slowed, a wave sent out from our bow rippled through the riffraff before us. Another bell tolled and with a whoosh of released steam, the boilers shut down. Except for the constant splash made by the lagging paddle wheel, *Diana* glided across the black water in silence. The captain gave the order for a hard turn to starboard. Within seconds, the pilot slipped *Diana* into a space between two steamboats that appeared along the shoreline, her shallow hull crunching against the riverbed. From the levee, a drayman announced our arrival and to prepare for offloading. Several wagons, their drivers, and slaves waited on Front

Street for us to finish landing. As soon as we stopped, out went the gangplanks and the crew immediately began to walk packs of furs onto shore. The drayman ceased his call.

I exited the dining room out to the main deck and worked my way down the gangplank. A small travel case given to me by Dr. Keynes held my belongings. Wearing only his loaned clothes and my brother's knife hidden under a coat, I felt unprotected, naked without buckskins and a pistol.

Billy followed the last of the packs carried off the steamer, met me on the levee and we walked up to Front Street. There was no hotel in the city but he knew a couple of establishments where a man might find a drink and a bed. One of the slaves glanced up at us from the back of a loaded wagon then looked to the ground. His foreman hit the side rail twice with the butt of a whip and the wagon lurched forward. The slave walked behind on bare feet with no chains binding him. Billy stopped and watched them disappear around a corner. Grimacing, he said under his breath, "Bloody Yanks . . ." and stood staring up the crowded street. An instant later, he slapped me on the back and set off at a quick pace.

"Come on then, mate, two pints er a callin' us to Frenchy's and I know who's a payin'!"

I walked slowly after him, trying to remember where I heard the name Frenchy. Then it came to me. That night on the river, as Baumgartner pulled Jonathan's tomahawk out of Jeffery's skull and handed it to Rudy, there was something said about Frenchy and St. Louis. I caught up and we strolled on into the heart of the city.

By darkness, all the buildings looked the same. Though the streets ran mostly straight and crossed each other at equal distances, I became thoroughly lost. Billy seemed to know precisely where we were and where he was taking us. I struggled to keep up with him through crowds of city folk who seemed to wander about aimlessly.

"Mate, can't be too different from Chicago," he said over his shoulder, then disappeared into a crowd of river rogues, trappers, and gentlemen gamblers. I pushed through the lot to stand next to Billy. Above us, on a balcony lit with torches, three women dressed in what seemed the latest fashions flirted with the men down on the street. Between the first and second floors of the building, a fancily drawn sign read, *Frenchy's Emporium.*

"This be the place, mate!" Billy yelled

above the din.

"Yes, I certainly hope so!" I yelled back, slapping him on the shoulder. We stepped onto the porch and through the open double doors. This time, Billy followed me.

A grizzly of a man halted us inside the lobby. Without looking up, he mumbled something about a search, reached inside my coat, and felt the knife. Then seeing my face for the first time, he seemed shocked and slowly pulled away, his hand empty. I passed, with him still staring at me. He tipped his hat to Billy and let him pass without a search.

"Mate, a pint for the both of us and to find Frenchy, the bastard owes me!" Billy hollered and made his way toward the bar. I stood overwhelmed by the mix of months-old sweat, cigar smoke and lavender perfume that hung in the air. This house was not only for a gentleman but for every river rat who had a few dollars to spend on a drink and a whore. As I followed Billy to the bar, a fair belle dressed in red silk and blonde braids took my hand. She frowned as I snatched it away. I was not there for a buck in the bed.

We toasted to a long friendship, though we had met only three days before. The warm beer tasted terrible but I drank anyway. With our backs to the bar, Billy eyed a couple of game tables in the corner under the stairs and I looked for a tall man with little hair and perfect teeth. I knew that if I found Baumgartner, Rudy might be close.

There came a clamor from the second-floor landing. The blonde braided girl took a tumble head first down the stairs to lay splayed across the floor, bleeding from her head. The room grew quiet as her temporary suitor slowly stomped down to her side. A large man he was, thick-headed and filthy, leaned in and pointed a finger at her face. "I come all the way from Minnesota, bringin' timber down river an' ain't never been stolen from yet. Ain't gonna be the first!" As she tried to sit up, he hit her in the nose, sending blood in every direction. She did not utter a sound.

I already had my knife pulled when Billy raised an arm to stop me. "Best these things work themselves out," he said and leaned back against the bar smiling. "Think of this as part of the show."

The grizzly man from the lobby moved through the crowd quick and swung a small club, hitting the back of the man's head. With a crack, he fell directly on top of the woman, smothering her. She somehow pushed off his motionless body and stood, pulling down her dress to cover her naked legs. While holding her bloody nose with one hand, she took the club from Grizzly and hit the man twice, on his shoulder and across his right hand. "Piece a shit ya are!" she yelled as blood streamed from her nose and head.

At the end of the bar, a door opened and a man stepped casually into the room. The bustling crowd again fell silent.

"Now the evening begins proper . . ." Billy whispered.

The man was dressed in a white satin shirt, drawn tight by a shiny leather belt. He wore black pantaloons tucked into knee boots. Graying black hair flowed free to the middle of his back and he wore a swirling mustache that seemed pasted on, yet fit impeccably with the contours of his handsome face. A scar as thick as a gold eagle coin ran across his chin and down his tattooed neck. Deep blue eyes matched the color of the scar. He portrayed a stunning figure of a man, a pirate without a patch or a musketeer without his feathered hat.

I began to laugh. Billy hit my ribs with his elbow, leaned in, and said, "Don't, else you might live to regret it."

I shut up.

"You, sir, are out of line," the man said loudly, drawing an ornately handled cutlass from its scabbard hanging about his waist. He walked slowly through the crowd, his blade parting the way.

Now awake, the river man laughed at the musketeer strolling toward him. He tried standing then yelped as he realized all the knuckles on his right hand must have been broken. A glazed look of pain turned to fear as the tip of a sword touched his throat.

"Ah, yes, out of line you are, sir, accusing my Christine, my beautiful *Fille de Joie,* that she steals from you. When you say this, it is as if you say . . ." He paused, pressing the blade closer. "I steal from you, *oui*?"

"No, no, sir, you ain't stolen nothin' from me. It was clearly her doin's, not yours." The river man sat up cross-legged and tried leaning back on his hands but could only balance on one. "Anyway," he said, his fear turning to anger, "what's it to you, ya goddamn dandy?"

The musketeer swung his cutlass, slicing the man's shirt and chest but not knocking him back. He then pulled a handkerchief from inside his shirtsleeve and dangled it in front of the bleeding man. Jerking it out of his reach, he handed it to Christine. She curtsied and clumsily wiped her bloody nose.

"I say again, sir, you accuse her, you accuse me."

The look on the man's face showed not anger now but panic. He uncrossed his legs and began pushing himself backward until his head hit a post in the middle of the floor. "Who, who are you?" he whined.

"Why, I am Frenchy," the musketeer declared, "of Frenchy's Emporium. Do you not even know where you lie, in a puddle of your own piss?" Then calmly, he asked, "Who the fuck er you?"

"John, sir, John Brigham."

"Well, John Brigham, one chance you have to redeem yourself tonight, to wash mine and Christine's good names clean of the accusations you so callously threw our way."

"Please, sir, I beg ya, let me walk. I meant nothin' by it. I got a wife an' three boys way north a here in Minnesota to go back to, after the timber's sold." With the sword back at his throat, he dropped his chin, almost touching its blade.

"Ladies and gentlemen, by the point and swipe of my sword does his tune change." Frenchy glared down at the man. "A wife and three boys? When he is away, do they know their father frequents whorehouses?"

Lifting the sword's blade, he raised John Brigham's chin back up to look him in the eye. "A disgrace you are, sir, to your family and this institution." Frenchy paused, as if to relish the silence of his tavern. With the flourish of a hand, he exclaimed, "To the pit I say, for your attempt at redemption!"

A roar of applause thundered through the room as Grizzly lifted John Brigham up to his feet. Behind the stairs, hidden, double doors flung open and he stumbled into darkness.

A young girl with nappy hair, pale skin, and the blackest of eyes stepped through the crowd of men toward Billy and me. She handed us each a small square piece of parchment and turned to walk away. She paused with a glance back, as if she recognized something about me, then was gone.

"Ah, mate, tonight's special. You meet Frenchy's pets." Billy smiled and with a wink, he finished his pint.

Chapter 12

The large parlor behind the stairs smelled of rotted meat and shit. Small oil lamps hung randomly on the walls between crooked paintings of young nymphs in various stages of undress. The ceiling had a smoke hole to the sky, black with the night. I felt a slight cross-breeze, as if someone had left an outside door cracked open. This did not relieve the room of its smell.

Thirty or so invited men crowded in and circled around a jagged hole sawed out of the floorboards fifteen or twenty feet across. There were no handrails and the creaking wood was worn slick at the edges. Billy Frieze somehow positioned me to stand next to Frenchy. He glanced at Billy and said nothing. Grizzly closed and locked the double doors, shutting out the noise of the tavern. In the quiet, I heard purrs and grunts hollowing up from below, sounding eerily familiar. I cautiously peered down into the pit and could see nothing. Then I heard the heavy breathing of a man.

"John Brigham, are you down there?" Frenchy yelled out with a grin. "We are in for a treat this very evening, John Brigham."

Grizzly lit a torch with one of the oil lamps and tossed it into the pit. The flame trailed ten feet down into the darkness and with a thud, the torch landed on the ground. Brigham tried picking it up with his right hand but could not because of his broken knuckles. With his left hand, he swung the fire in a panic, as any white man from Minnesota would do when hearing those particular animal noises.

"Chase your own shadow, do you, John Brigham?" Frenchy exclaimed to all. "I sense you know my northern pets by their laughter, *oui*?"

Brigham swung the torch to his left, then to his right, leaving arcs of fire to brighten the pit. He seemed baffled as to where the grunts and growls came from. He became still and held the torch above his head, staring up at Frenchy and his invited guests. "I know whatcha ya got comin', you bastard." He paused to wipe sweat out of his eyes and from his brow. "I'll burn its eyes out, then cook an' eat it."

Someone sloshed a drink down onto the

torch. The entire pit flashed bright as the fire lit the whiskey, exposing a hole in the wall, close to the ground and covered with bars. Brigham shielded himself from the spray of fire and randomly swept the torch toward the opening. A weasel-like snout poked through the cover, then disappeared. The grunts became louder and deeper as the animal appeared again and began to chew furiously on one of the iron bars. The river man from Minnesota held the fire close to the hole, hunched over into a crouch, and screamed at the top of his voice "Ugh, Ugh . . . !"

Everyone laughed, except for Frenchy and me. He leaned in close and asked, "You witness a trial such as this before now?"

I turned my head, locking eyes with him. His cold stare bore into me. He shifted his attention slightly to my left cheek then back to my gaze, not blinking once.

"I know a wolverine well," I said calmly, shifting my gaze to the blue scar on his chin.

"My new friend, I'm sure you do . . ." He paused, as if to say something more, then leaned in closer and whispered, "Wolverines."

Brigham stopped screaming, then *bam*. A piercing yelp and sharp cracks of breaking teeth and bone echoed up from the pit, making us all jump. Brigham had slammed the torch against the cover, hitting the beast square in the snout as it gnawed on the bar. Grizzly kneeled, reached down past the floorboards, and heaved on a chain hanging above the opening. With a hair-raising scrape, the bars slid up. A growling black shadow, the size of a small wolf, streaked to the far wall and disappeared in the dark. Brigham swung the torch too late to stop the wolverine from tearing into the left side of his groin. He wheezed in a breath but could not exhale. With the few sharp teeth it had left, the animal thrashed sideways, letting go only to take better bites. Brigham flipped the torch upside down and with one hand shoved the fire into its eyes, bashing its head repeatedly. The blind and badly beaten wolverine tore away, with muscle and tendon clenched in its teeth. Brigham staggered back against the wall and slumped down, laying the torch in his pooling blood. With a sizzle, the fire went out.

The acrid, sulfur smell of burnt fur filled the parlor. Grunts and whimpers drifted up from the pit and stopped with one last gasped breath.

Brigham groaned, then hollered up, "I killed yer goddamned pet, you bastard, now I'm gonna eat it!"

"*Oui,* and at what price you pay? Soon you will be dead from your bleeding." Frenchy leaned over and peered down into the darkness. The ragged edge of the floorboards creaked as everyone else followed suit. Partially covered by his hair, the look on Frenchy's face, it seemed, was one of mild disappointment.

Grizzly lit another torch and tossed it down.

"Hurt but sure ain't dyin'!" Brigham declared, sounding stronger. He picked up the torch and stood right below Frenchy. Piss, shit, and blood soaked his britches. He had somehow torn a piece of shirt and tied a tourniquet around his leg to slow down the bleeding. Broken knuckles caused the fingers on his right hand to curl up inside his wrist. Otherwise, John Brigham was very much alive.

Noise seeped through the double doors that led back into the tavern. Women's laughter interrupted the seriousness of this affair. I breathed a sigh, relieved that John Brigham would live. I had experienced enough for one day and night, was bone tired and ready to find a bed to sleep in. The evening had taken a wild turn. I could not have imagined Billy Frieze leading me to stand over a pit of darkness, enclosing a man torn apart by a wolverine, yet still alive. Though I questioned why I stood on slick, creaky boards overlooking the justifiably defiant man, I was happy to be standing next to the one who might lead me to Rudy and Baumgartner. I learned long ago not to question Providence, no matter the brutality of the situation.

Frenchy began to chuckle, softly at first, through his nose, almost a snort. He stopped, then burst into a gut-wrenching laugh. One by one, the others began to laugh, as if catching a joke to which I was not privy.

A deep growl echoed out of the hole in the wall. A second beast attacked with vicious speed and strength, nearly knocking Brigham to the ground.

The son-of-a-bitch did indeed have more than one wolverine!

Frenchy turned to me and saw I was not laughing with him and his friends. I stared into his cold eyes, leaned in close, and hissed, "Brigham paid yer goddamn price."

He shoved me into the man at my right, which knocked him into the next man, and him into the next man. We all teetered at the edge of the floorboards.

"Did I not say animals? My pets? Two pets from the north!" Frenchy bellowed, then looked straight at me. "You do not trust what I say?"

I leaped into the pit.

With a jar, I landed upright in the shadows, knife drawn.

The wolverine darted in, chomping onto Brigham's right hand, shaking it, then darting back, out of the way of the torch. His swings became useless as the animal continued to tear at his hand and arm, pulling him to the ground to get at his throat. By the fire, I saw him lose three fingers. The tourniquet ceased working, blood streamed from his torn groin to pool on the sticky ground.

John Brigham was dying.

I stepped between the two. The wolverine backed away grunting, licking its bloody teeth. Brigham stumbled forward, nearly knocking me down. He took a half-hearted swing at my head then fell, face first to the ground. I snatched up the torch and inched toward the animal, flushing it away from the hole so there was no escape.

"How dare you interfere with my justice!" Frenchy screamed.

I did not look up at him. The only sound heard was the wolverine's rapid purring, as it paced back and forth in front of me. The boards above my head were quiet.

"Who in hell have you brought to me, Billy Frieze?"

"He seems to be a friend of Rudy's, mate."

"*Oui,* his cheek, with the scar?" Frenchy sighed. "What is his name, *mate?*" he mimicked.

"Zebadiah Creed, if it is indeed his true name," Billy said calmly. The rest of the men stood silent; the wolverine stopped pacing.

Frenchy peered down at me. "*Jebadiah* Creed, eh. We shall see who you really are!"

"Zebadiah," I whispered and set the torch down.

The wolverine attacked, swift and silent.

With a fist full of fur, I embraced the beast, rolled backward, and drove my knife through its heart. Letting go, I sent it slamming against the wall. Frenchy's pet slid to the ground, dead, without a whimper.

No one above me spoke a word. It seemed even the tavern fell silent.

Brigham was still alive. He had turned over to lie on his back. Holding the torch, I kneeled next to him as he moaned, then tried to talk.

". . . an' tell them boys a' mine I'm sorry." He paused to lick his lips then seemed to stare right through me. "I see stars," he whispered. I glanced up, past Frenchy and the shadowed spectators to three stars shining through the smoke hole in the ceiling. I looked back down at Brigham. He smiled then grimaced. "I shoulda killed the whore."

With his last breath, I began to sing a death song. The Lakota words comforted me as I knelt beside a pool of blood seeping into the earthen ground. For an instant, I felt a shift in the air, barely perceptible, more a feeling perhaps than real.

Frenchy's long, black hair nearly covered his face as he leaned over the pit. With the shadow of a smile, he seemed in awe of what he had witnessed. He turned to Grizzly and nodded. Grizzly raised a short, fat gun, its barrel opening wide to a funnel. I had not seen a blunderbuss since my brief stay at Fort Union.

"You sing John Brigham's death song, why?" Frenchy asked.

"He died fightin'."

"And if he had not fought bravely, would you still sing his song?"

"Yes."

"A compassionate man you are, *Jebadiah* Creed."

"My name is Zebadiah . . .."

Frenchy waved a hand to Grizzly. "Whatever is your name, this is not a place for compassion my friend."

I raised my arms to cover my face and heard the click of the flintlock, then a deafening *sha-boom*.

The world went black.

CHAPTER 13

I stand alone at the rudder, guiding a half-submerged keelboat through the hidden shoals and sandbars of a mighty flowing river. There are no shorelines as water and sky merge into one, open space. Yet, I feel constricted, confined to one course, determined to reach my destination. Jonathan pops his head out of the water then rises up to stand on its rippling surface. He strolls toward me leaving footprints in his wake. As we pass each other, not a word is spoken, no acknowledgment but for a nod.

I smelled burnt acorns and lavender perfume.

The late-afternoon sun shone through a window beside the bed. Blue curtains fluttered in a cool breeze with a bare hint of autumn in the air. Outside, I heard children laughing, playing a game, calling to one another who tagged whom and who was out. The bed I lay in was soft, not a thin bunk on a steamboat or a hay-stuffed mattress, but a real bed with shiny, gold sheets and pillows. I lay naked and clean, as if I had a wash. The pounding in the back of my head reminded me of how I came to be in that room.

The woman turned away from the window. My heart skipped a beat or two. Framed by the sun, with curly, blonde hair hung to her shoulders, I thought she was Anna.

"You sleep long."

She leaned forward, enough for me to see her face and to know she was not Anna. Her accented voice sounded hollow, toneless because of her broken nose. She had no bandages and no one had set the break. The two black eyes and bruises would eventually disappear, but her nose would always be crooked to the left. I tried not to show my disappointment and distrust upon recognizing her as the woman from the evening before.

"Frenchy says, 'My new friend, take good care of him, eh, Christine?' I say to Frenchy, he is beat to shit pretty good." She laughed, high and whiny. "But I know the man who hit my nose, and much worse is he than you!" I did not flinch as she reached over and gently touched my right shoulder where the hole used to be. She traced a finger along the scars on my chest, barely visible now because of the small welts and bruises that peppered my upper body. Whatever Grizzly shot me with certainly did not kill me, but it hurt, as if being hit by a raging hailstorm. I still smelled burnt acorns.

"Frenchy says you are one lucky buck you ain't dead." She paused to glance back out the window. The children had gone elsewhere to play. "He must like you. Most folks he don't like, 'round here anyhow."

"Where are my clothes?" I covered up to my waist with the sheet.

"Your clothes are no good after you been shot. I will fetch others."

"I had a travel case . . ."

She turned back to me, then glanced away again without looking me in the eye. "I know nothing 'bout a case."

She reached over and, with a finger, touched the scar on my left cheek, then jerked away and stuck the finger in her mouth, as if to cool it from a burn. She strode to the door and opened it. I heard a chair scrape the floor. Grizzly poked his head into the room. He gazed at his handiwork on my chest and arms, grinned, and stepped back.

"Frenchy says, 'Christine, you ain't no good for whorin' now, with a broke nose. You keep my new friend comp'ny,' 'n he gives me a wink." She glanced down at the outline of my pecker under the sheet and smiled. "Later, I come back with clothes. But you don't be too hasty gettin' into yer britches, eh?"

"How 'bout some food?" I had not eaten since leaving *Diana* the evening before.

"Sapphire will bring your supper," Christine said and walked out, leaving a lingering smell of perfume. The door locked behind her.

I needed to piss badly and searched for a chamber pot. Finding none, I pissed out the window onto the now busy street. I did not much care if anyone below me was soiled.

I lay back for a long while, watching the flutter of the curtains. Though I was obviously being held prisoner, I was glad to be alive. If I was shot at any closer range, no matter what filled the barrel of the gun, I would be dead. I thought of John Brigham. A man with much to lose died by his own willful conceit and pride, at the play of another man's stronger conceit and power. The stark brutality of the situation did not surprise me for I had experienced this many times on the north plains. Folks died for all kinds of reasons, some deserving and some not. I was not sure why I jumped. Brigham was on his way to being dead as soon as the second wolverine attacked. The truth was, I could not help myself. Anna was right, I stood down in that pit as genuine as ever, no matter the clothes I wore.

I felt bad for losing the doctor's travel case; inside were my buckskins and pistol. Right then, I wished to be wearing them.

The lock turned and in through the door stepped the young, nappy-haired Negress. She placed a plate of carrots and potatoes mixed with thick strips of venison and gravy onto a table at the foot of the bed. Alongside supper, she set a glass of beer and a knife and fork.

"Thank you," I said and got out of bed, letting the sheet fall to the floor. Sapphire turned away as if embarrassed. She must have been all of twelve or thirteen years old.

I wrapped the sheet around me, went to the door, and opened it wider. Grizzly immediately stood and blocked my way out of the room. The narrow hall was already lit with candles for the evening. Again, I smelled lavender perfume.

"Mr. Frenchy has invited you to a drink in his private sitting room." Grizzly sounded

113

as if he was a man of distinction and not a mudsill as he represented himself with his common dress. "Of course, after your supper, sir. Miss Christine will return with suitable clothing for you."

"What's your name, mister?" Though I felt uncomfortable standing next to him, I was not going to show any lack of confidence.

"Gerard, sir, my name is Gerard."

"Well, Gerard, I suppose I should thank you for not killin' me. If I may ask, what shot did ya scatter me with?"

He smiled, barely showing teeth through his ragged beard. "Acorns, sir. A barrel full of acorns with only twenty-five grains of powder will stop a bear in its tracks, but won't kill the thing."

"I knew it!" I exclaimed, slapping my thigh, genuinely pleased with myself. No matter that he bruised most of my body with his shot and probably nearly killed me, I respected the way he went about it.

Still standing at the doorway wrapped in a sheet, I looked back at the food on the table. Sapphire had placed a chair and waited with a napkin in her hand staring at me. I sat down and ate. Figuring I would not make a run for it, Gerard left the door open. I had all the luxuries of an honored guest, except for my freedom.

After sundown, Christine brought me clothes. I was as embarrassed wearing them as I was standing naked. The billowy, white silk shirt fit proper, with the pants feeling a little too tight. A black belt and boots finished me. All I needed was a cutlass hanging from my waist and I might as well have been Frenchy's brother.

"*Oui, Monsieur,* how handsome you look!" she exclaimed, clapping her hands.

"Why, thank you, my dear." I attempted to bow and realized how much pain I was in from the acorn shot. I also needed to piss again, and to sit for a while in the privy.

"Frenchy is waiting, *Jebadiah.*"

I gave her a stern glance. "Zebadiah."

"Is what I said, *Jebadiah.* Now you go to Frenchy."

I sighed and followed her out of the room. Gerard was not at the door.

Christine led me through candlelit halls, with closed doors on each side. It being early in the evening, I guessed Frenchy's whores were not that busy, else there would be more comings and goings with their customers. After the second turn, we came to a dark hall with one door at the end. A string hung out of a tiny hole in the ceiling. Christine pulled on the stick tied to the end and somewhere in a room above us, a bell

115

rang out a single, muffled note. We waited. She reached up, straightened the collar of my shirt, then patted my chest, as Anna had done not a week before.

The same bell tolled once again.

"Ready for you, Frenchy is."

She pulled the door open, curtsied, and walked back the way we came.

Before me was a tiny platform, a landing of sorts for the most unusual staircase I had ever seen. The dimly lit room was round, with wood steps built into the wall. Every step to my right led down and curved to the left, into darkness. Every step to my left would take me up and curve to the right to end, I presumed by the location of the ringing bell, at the door of Frenchy's sitting room. I inched out to the rough edge of the landing and looked up, then down. The whole staircase was a swirl, a thin twig wrapped loosely around a finger from the knuckle to the tip. It reminded me of the insides of snail shells.

Counting twelve steps up, I came to a door and pressed my ear to the wood. I heard murmurs, spoken in French, then laughter, and then someone speaking English, almost a recitation. I stood very still, my heart pounding.

I would be dead had Frenchy not seen

some favor in me. I killed his wolverine and in St. Louis, they were certainly hard to come by. I stole away the climax of Brigham's trial in front of his invited guests, yet he spared my life. So what might my sense of justice be to him, insanity? On impulse I jumped to save a dead man, was that not an insane act? I knew all too well that I could surely die by Frenchy's hand or Gerard's. Yet, justice and insanity might be one in the same. To clear his name, Brigham survived one wolverine attack, only to be torn apart by a second one. Still, by his last dying breath, he wished to have killed the whore. Back at the tavern, Frenchy seemed to know this about Brigham, even before his cutlass sliced the man's chest.

In some strange way, I felt a kin to the man I was about to have a drink with. Or, by his hand, be killed.

I knocked on the door.

"Entrer!" Someone called out. The door swung open, as if on its own.

Dozens of candles lit up a narrow room, as bright as if the sun had not yet set. I stood in the darkness of the stairwell adjusting to the light. The only wall adornment was a tapestry hung opposite the door, as intricate as any painting I had ever seen, with two great war ships side-by-side firing upon each other. Only one flew a flag and it was black. Windows built into the right side of the low, vaulted ceiling were propped open to let in the early autumn chill. Frenchy and Gerard sat opposite each other, in the middle of the room, on two halves of a rum barrel turned upside down, on bright, red pillows. Gerard held a book in his hand, reading aloud to Frenchy.

". . . The savage spurned the worthless rags, and perceiving that the shawl had already become a prize to another, his bantering but sullen smile changing to a gleam of ferocity, he dashed the head of the infant against a rock, and cast its quivering remains to her feet. For an instant the mother stood, like a statue of despair, looking wildly down at the unseemly object, which had so lately nestled in her bosom and smiled in her face; and then raised her eyes and countenance toward heaven, as if calling on God to curse the perpetrator of the foul deed."

Gerard stopped reading and with a finger holding his place, closed the book. Frenchy sat still with his hands in his lap. They both seemed unaware of me standing outside the open door. I cleared my throat, twice.

"Ah, *Monsieur Jebadiah,* do come in." Frenchy rose and offered a handshake. I

118

stepped into the room and extended my hand. Though I felt a true sense of confidence in his firm grip, he held on a little too long. We locked eyes. Again, for an instant, I felt a cold heart dwelling somewhere deep inside him. Then he smiled and the feeling was gone.

"You are well dressed and bathed I see. Christine, my lovely, broken flower, takes good care of you, *no*?" Gerard stood and moved away from the half-barrel. Frenchy offered me the seat.

"Yes, sir. Bruised, but I will heal." I glanced at Gerard as he rocked back and forth on his heels, holding the book behind his back.

"*Oui,* a good shot Gerard is, though an expert at what load will kill a man or only knock him down."

Gerard smiled at this.

"He is a much better reader of English than me. You do read, *Monsieur Jebadiah,* don't you?"

I could not tell if he mispronounced my name on purpose, or he simply could not say it correctly. I decided this was not the time or place to make it a concern.

"Yes, sir, I do read English . . ." I paused. Then added, "And French."

"You know James Fenimore Cooper, then?"

"No," I said rather abruptly, as I was not expecting to be quarried about my reading prowess or knowledge of authors.

"Gerard, allow *Monsieur Jebadiah* a chance to finish the passage."

Gerard handed me the book, open to the page where he left off, and pointed to a paragraph. I turned to the front cover. I did not know the book *The Last of the Mohicans.* The words on the page spun in circles until I was able to focus.

I began reading, stuttering. ". . . She was spared the sin of such a prayer; for, maddened at his disappointment, and excited at the sight of blood, the Huron mercifully drove his tomahawk into her own brain. The mother sank under the blow, and fell, grasping at her child, in death, with the same engrossing love that had caused her to cherish it when living."

I stopped reading. Gerard continued to rock silently back and forth.

"Goddamn savages . . ." Frenchy whispered with his eyes closed.

Two light taps came at the door. He hollered out, *"Entrer!"* and in walked Sapphire, the young Negress, carrying my travel case. She laid it in my lap and stood next to

Frenchy.

"Merci, ma fille douce," he said and gave her a gentle hug. She looked down as if embarrassed, smiled and moved closer into his shoulder, then stared at me with her black eyes.

"Your daughter?" I asked.

"Oui. Her mother, some say, is a . . ." He turned to Gerard. *"Comment dite-vous sorcière?"*

"Witch."

"Witch," Frenchy repeated. "A spell she spins and see what she gives to me!" He pressed his daughter close and kissed her cheek. All the while, she continued to stare at me then the travel case.

"Père, the contents are his but not the box."

"Ah. Shall we see what he has hidden in the box, my dear *fille?"*

Sapphire simply nodded.

"You do like surprises, *oui, Monsieur Jebadiah?"* They both waited for my answer.

It seemed Gerard moved toward me but stayed in place, rocking back and forth. I gave him the book. As he again held it behind his back, I suspected the book was not all he had in his hands.

I reached down and slowly unhooked both latches. I flung open the travel case. Lying on top of folded buckskins was my brother's elk-handled knife. The same bloody, dust-covered knife I killed the wolverine with the night before. I wanted to pick it up but hesitated. Instead, I lifted the clothes to peek at the bundle Anna had given me, and the pistol with the shooting bag. Seeing them gave me little comfort. I touched the handle of the knife and remembered the dream I had a few hours before, Jonathan rising from the water, but for a nod, not a word said to me.

"Père, le couteau nèst pas le son," Sapphire whispered under her breath.

"What do you say, my sweet?" Her father cocked his head toward her, as if thinking about what she had said. Then, "The knife is someone else's?"

"The knife is his brother's, or was," she said clearly, in English, continuing to give me her hypnotic stare.

The travel case nearly slipped from my lap, the knife sliding off the buckskins onto the pistol with a clink. My hands trembled as I laid it back square on the buckskins. I could not conceal my surprise and stark bewilderment. She seemed to know my thoughts and dreams.

Frenchy laughed, as he had the night before, loud and bold. "I tell you, *Monsieur*

Jebadiah, she is more her mother's daughter every day."

As quick as he began, he stopped laughing. With a finger, he slowly traced the scar on his chin down to the dark red neck tattoo.

Gerard ceased his rocking. The air in the room dropped several degrees.

"Who are you, *Monsieur* Creed?" Frenchy asked.

I lowered my head. A drop of sweat landed on the knife blade, diluting the wolverines' dried blood.

"Sir, I am Zebadiah Creed."

"*Monsieur,* I have a name. This tells me nothing." He leaned across and placed a boot between mine. "Who are you?"

"I am Zebadiah Creed, fur trapper." I took a deep breath and raised my head. With one swipe, I could have easily cut his throat.

"And Lakota warrior."

Frenchy jerked his boot away, slapped his thigh, and shouted, "I knew it! *Monsieur Jebadiah,* a warrior you are." He again jammed his boot between mine and with an arm still around Sapphire, leaned forward. "But are you savage?"

In a daze, I stared at him, then at his black-eyed daughter, and did not answer.

He glanced at Gerard and said, "We go

downstairs now," then pointed to my left cheek. "Before this evening is finished, you will tell of your scar, *oui*?" He slowly stroked his chin. "And I will tell of mine."

I closed and latched the travel case, leaving the knife be.

CHAPTER 14

In the dim light, I saw Billy Frieze's face turn pale as an old, sun-weathered bone.

Frenchy gave a slight smile. "I thought he be dead too, *mate.*" He shrugged and glanced back to Gerard, standing with his back to the door we had walked through. With a wink, he said, "My man's shot is not as powerful as he would like to believe."

I stood next to Frenchy, adjusting to the light of a roaring fire at the opposite end of a cavernous room. A massive stone fireplace stood two stories high, with narrow, open windows on each side. A huge tapestry hung on the wall, similar to the one in the sitting room upstairs. By the flicker of the fire, I saw what appeared to be the same two ships mixed in explosive battle.

Stepping before us, Billy seemed recovered enough to stretch out a hand. "Mighty damn glad for you to be alive, mate."

I shook his hand. "Mighty damn glad

myself."

To Frenchy he said, "Been waiting down here for an hour or more, mate." He looked me up and down. "He wears your boots well."

Frenchy shrugged again and strolled on into the room. At the fire, he lit several torches and set them in holders scattered about the cluttered floor. With his hands on his hips, he proudly announced, "*Monsieur* Creed, welcome to my museum."

The room lit up, illuminating various large, strange structures made of wood and iron. One of them was a platform with rope strung through iron rings and two large wheels attached. Another contraption, maybe ten feet high and covered with white cloth, stood like a ghost near the right wall. Laid out on three tables were implements of war, everything from bows, arrows, and spears to swords, tomahawks, and knives. Many styles and embellishments I had never seen.

There were no pistols or rifles.

"Everyone thinks you are dead, the talk of St. Louis, mate." Billy stared at me. "You must be hurtin' by the blast of that gun . . ."

"Might like bein' dead for awhile. This bruised ghost could spook a couple a fellas I'm lookin' for," I said.

Frenchy listened with his head hung, then looked up. "And might one of these fellas go by the name Rudy? Among other names I've heard him called." He paused, "The same bastard who gave you the cut on your cheek?"

I glanced to Billy. "This slight cut seems to be looked upon as somethin' known about by a lot of folks. An' I'm the one left out a' knowin' . . ."

Both of them smiled at each other, then at me.

"Mate, what's amazing is that you ain't died twice, first by Rudy's knife and then by Gerard's thunder gun."

"One lucky son-of-bitch you are." Frenchy snickered. "No matter, you are now with friends." He raised an eyebrow. "To whom you must tell the tale that brought you to stand here this evening."

"Ah, but first, might we have that drink you promised?" Billy said, licking his lips.

Frenchy strode back to the fireplace, threw on a couple of logs, and gestured for us to sit on stools. The windows let in cool evening air to mix with the warmth of the fire. Frenchy poured us drinks. This evening had been well prepared for.

I told them everything, from the fight with Fitzpatrick and Fontenelle up at the Green

River Rendezvous and the bushwhacking by Jeffery, Rudy, and Baumgartner, to the time spent healing with Dr. Keynes and his daughter. I did not mention my affair with Anna. It was not their business.

Afterward, I felt drained, as if most of those memories I kept bottled tight inside were poured into the fire and burned up. I was relieved, but I dared not show it to my two new friends.

"Baumgartner, eh?" Frenchy shot a glance at Billy.

"Eh, mate, a good man once, until . . ." Billy exclaimed.

Frenchy sat quiet for a second and then answered, ". . . Until Benjamin Brody."

"Benjamin Brody, a Brit livin' in New Orleans?" I asked. "Baumgartner mentioned him, before he shot my brother. Probably figured we both would be dead so no matter to say his name. And now you bring him up?"

But for the crackling of the fire, a heavy silence filled the room. I did not know if I had said too much.

At last, Frenchy spoke. "A tale I will tell you now, *Monsieur Jebadiah.*" He stood and beckoned me to join him at a table covered with knives and swords. He picked up a rather plain looking long knife and held it to the firelight. The glint off the steel blade matched the shine in his eyes.

"This is what cut me . . ." He ran a finger across the blade then traced the tip from his upper chin down to the red tattoo on the right side of his neck. He stared absently into the fire with a slight grin, as if he enjoyed reenacting the cut. His stare grew cold and blue as the scar. "By the hand of Brody."

He spat on the floor then gave me the knife. The slightly curved blade and oak handle were in precise balance, a design to slice under a ribcage and cut out a bear's heart. A hint of blood stained the guard.

"Betrayed by a woman, I was. But, it was Brody. He cut me up enough, but not dead." He jerked back his shirt to reveal that the scar continued down to the center of his chest. "She wanted my heart, but he did not have the . . ." Frenchy turned to Gerard. *"Comment vous dire courage?"*

"Courage."

"Oui, he did not have the courage to cut out my heart. Yet, I leave my life *en disgrâce,* with only a *petit bébé* bundled in my arms, and this scar. Eleven years I raise the child." He held his arms up wide and spun in a slow circle. "I was the king of Louisiana, my Barataria, and all the warm waters of the

Caribbean. I come here, I build this from nothing in St. Louie, Frenchy's Emporium."

He stopped spinning and faced me. My bewilderment must have shown as disbelief for he frowned and slowly closed his shirt, covering the lower portion of his scar.

Frenchy's voice became a low growl. "You, my new friend, will take that knife you hold in your hand to New Orleans and avenge the loss of my legacy."

I shook my head as my bewilderment turned to incomprehension.

"I am no assassin."

He stepped closer. "Ah, *Monsieur . . . Jebadiah,* one is only an assassin if he is paid." His blue eyes sparkled as his upper lip and mustache trembled. "You, sir, owe me a life."

I stepped backward, bumping the table and rattling the blades of the knives and swords. "How is this?"

"You killed my precious Pepe."

"Who, who the hell is Pepe?"

He gritted his teeth. "My precious pet, Pepe, my fucking wolverine."

I looked to Billy. He simply shook his head.

"So, I am to kill a man 'cause I owe you for killin' a goddamn wolverine?"

He took one step closer. We were almost

touching noses. I still held the knife in my hand.

"Oui."

I glanced over his shoulder and almost stumbled into him. On another table a few feet away, I recognized the very thing that drew me to this man in the first place.

"I'll do as you ask, but . . ." Gathering my strength, I leaned forward, inching him away. "You'll give me the tomahawk Rudy sold you."

Knowing exactly where it lay, he picked up Jonathan's tomahawk and flipped it to point the handle at my gut. Five scalps hung from two coup rings tied at the base of the blade.

"Yours it is, my friend."

I took hold of the handle. Frenchy held tight for a second, giving me his cold stare, and let go. He slowly turned back toward the fireplace, laughing.

"Another drink?" Billy asked.

Still leaning against the table, my shaking caused the blades and handles to jingle against one another. I held the knife in my right hand, it draining what strength and will I had that remained from the conversation. My brother's tomahawk hung from my left hand, its worn handle smooth, except for the death notches cut into the wood. I raised it up to the firelight, the blade clean of any blood and bone from Jeffery's skull. The hair of the scalps fluttered down, brushing across my fingers. Two were my brother's and three were mine. I placed the knife in my belt and with both hands swung the tomahawk loosely in a figure eight over and over again, the scalps singing through the air, until sweat beaded on my forehead. I stopped and cradled the blade gently in hand, rubbing my thumb across its sharp edge. Blood trickled to the floor. I held tears in my eyes, but I was no longer shaking.

All three men stared at me. Gerard still stood by the door. Billy took a drink, averting his eyes when I glanced at him. Frenchy, with hands on his hips, gave me the same gleaming look of awe as he had the evening before, after I killed his wolverine. In an instant, that look was gone.

I faced Billy and Frenchy.

"What of Baumgartner and Rudy?" I said quietly.

"Eh, mate, when Rudy's involved, things go bad quick." Billy shook his head. "Bloody bad. The cut on your face is found on dead men, not ones still living."

Frenchy smiled. "A true *meurtrier* he is, a master. Like I say, you one lucky buck for not being long dead by his knife."

"By your own words, holding back Rudy, Baumgartner saved yer life, mate."

From the corner of my eye, I saw something move. A canvas cover lay on a narrow board next to the tall, clothed contraption. The cover moved again. I heard a groan, then, "Oh, son-of-bitch!"

I recognized the voice and froze.

"Speak of the devil." Frenchy exclaimed. "My former partner awakes."

He jerked back the canvas, leaving Rudy blinking by the light of the fire.

The bastard was lying there the whole time!

In an instant, my memories came flooding back and I was on the river, that night, smelling the dogwood tree and mint, the smoke of the rifles, Rudy's whiskey breath. I felt Baumgartner's stinking top hat pushed down around my ears and the dull ache where the doctor pulled the ball from my shoulder. I heard the pistol shot in my ear, killing my brother.

I felt shame in my heart and hatred in my gut.

I stepped toward Rudy. My urge was to take the tomahawk I still held in my hand — the very tomahawk he bashed me in the head with — swing down, and kill him. It did not matter that his hands and feet were tied. Yet, I hesitated and turned back to

Billy. He gave me a nervous grin and shrugged.

"Trussed up like a pig, my old friend is . . ." Frenchy said as he stood next to me. He seemed pleased by my surprise and by my restraint.

"Why you done this, Frenchy?" Rudy slurred. "I been good with you."

"*Oui,* and yet you run, as the tide runs along south *Terre Bonne.*" Frenchy shook his head. "In, out, out and in. Though, because the saw grass always hides you, I cannot keep up with my old friend. One day, the grass will cut my feet, trip me, drag me down. The hidden tide rushes in to drown me, even here, way upriver in St. Louie."

As Frenchy spoke, Rudy's eyes glazed. Gerard stepped up to the other side of me, reached over, and slapped him, hard, on top of his head. Rudy yelped and then squirmed, trying to get out of his bonds. He almost fell to the floor and Gerard shoved him back onto the narrow piece of wood. It was then I noticed the board was attached to the tall, covered structure. Frenchy casually reached up and pulled on the cloth. It fell away to reveal two ten-foot-tall pieces of thick wood, connected at the top by a short piece, equally thick, with a large pulley hanging in between. A rope was strung through and tied to a brace, holding in place a steel blade cut at an angle. Below was a block for a person's head to fit in to. I had heard of this contraption. It was an ingenious way to kill someone. For a few short seconds, I stood wondering how it came to be in St. Louis.

"I ain't the buck ya want. Baumgartner, you want him, an' the shit Brit name of Brody. I made some side money is all, on them pelts," Rudy said, as a matter of fact. "Didn't make much, not like them other bastards makin'." Now much more alert, he stared up at the shiny blade. "I was always comin' back, Frenchy, you know . . ."

"Dead are Baumgartner and Brody." Frenchy gave me a quick sideways glance, as if I would say something. "The last one is you, Rudy." He paused. "Unless . . ."

Rudy noticed me. "I know you. The buck we stole from." He stopped, as if to collect his memory. Then his eyes grew wide. "We, we left you fer dead by that creek."

"Ain't dead now," I exclaimed, swinging Jonathan's tomahawk, as Rudy had the night he hit me.

Frenchy stepped in front of me with both hands in the air. "*Aucun, aucun!* You don't kill him yet!" He leaned in close to my ear and whispered, "Another question or two my new friend, Then . . ." His eyes gleamed with delight.

Gerard grabbed Rudy by the scruff of his smock and belt, flipped him over, face down, and shoved his head into the block. He pulled down the upper piece and latched it into place. Frenchy motioned Billy to bring him one of the stools and he sat down next to Rudy.

"Tell me what is to happen now," he calmly demanded, brushing the hair out of Rudy's eyes.

"I tell you nothing, you goddamn bastard, 'cause I already tell you everything."

"Who else is tied with you that is not dead?"

"I tell, you still cut off my head, you fucking prig."

Frenchy laughed and looked up. "If I cut off your head, you will not know. But, if you give me one name." He began to slowly untie the rope that held the blade in place. "One last chance I give to redeem, Rudy Dupree. One name, I tie the rope back and you take your chances with *Monsieur Jebadiah*." He let the rope slip. The blade slid down a couple of inches.

"Fitzpatrick! He set us up at Rendezvous. He knew they was goin' down the river alone. Easy takin' then sell to Brody in New Orleans, is where Baumgartner went. But you say them both are dead right?"

Frenchy turned to me then back to Rudy. "Soon enough, they'll be dead."

Rudy sighed and became very still. "Cut me loose. I'll kill the red nigger lover an' be on my way."

His face was turned sideways in the block. He watched as Frenchy finished untying the rope and handed it to me. The blade was surprisingly heavy to hold in place.

"Be done with him by letting go."

In one hand, I clutched a taut rope, from the other hung a tomahawk with five scalps. Rudy stared up at me. I saw no remorse, no fear, only disgust.

I handed the rope back to Frenchy and stepped into a fighting stance. "Cut him loose."

"An honorable man you are, *Monsieur* Zebadiah. However . . ." Frenchy stood up and stretched, then leaned down and looked Rudy in the eye. "I am not."

The rope slipped from his hand.

CHAPTER 15

No one sang a song for the dead man.

When Billy and I left Frenchy's museum by way of the staircase, Rudy's head was still in a basket below the guillotine. Gerard had begun to clean up the mess by covering the body and on his knees, scrubbed the drying blood off the floor with a brush and bucket of water. Frenchy sat on one of the stools, leaning forward staring into the fire, his long hair shadowing his face. Before leaving, Billy tried to gain his attention, but he sat silent, ignoring the both of us.

With the knife I was given to kill Brody still in my belt, I absently carried the tomahawk in hand through the halls back to my room, a few women and their customers scurrying to clear a path. Whispering began as soon as I passed. Not until I saw myself by candlelight in a small wall mirror did I realize my face and white shirt were spattered with blood.

I blew out all but one candle and sat quiet on the bed for a long while, staring out the open window, the moonless night somehow comforting. Though the late-evening air was not that cold, I could not stop shivering.

Around and around, blood thoughts swirled through my mind, the imagined fight to the death with a man I swore to kill. Rudy was the reason I left Anna, Rascal, and Dr. Keynes, leaving a peaceful life on the river behind. Rudy Dupree and Baumgartner were the only reasons for me to be in St. Louis, sitting on an empty bed in a whorehouse. The burn of indignation was not cooled by mere satisfaction that Rudy was dead. Yet, all I could see were his eyes staring up at me from the guillotine's basket. I slammed my fists down on the windowsill and howled with rage, tears seeping from my eyes. A couple of men down the street answered with their own howls, then yelps and laughter. I yelled back, "Go to hell, you sons of bitches!" Their laughter drifted away into the night.

The door swung open. I swiftly stood, pulling the knife from my belt. The bright glow of the hall candles cut a silhouette of Frenchy's daughter. She set my travel case on the bed.

"*Père* says you may go now."

She turned to leave, then stopped. Even as a silhouette, I could see her eyes, blacker than two shadows. "You will know my *mère* in New Orleans."

The door closed behind her with a click. I sat back down for a while longer, wondering what she meant by her last words.

I re-lit the room candles and washed my face, turning the water in the bowl red.

A little after midnight, I walked downstairs to the smoke-filled tavern, past the spot where the evening before John Brigham had hit Christine and met with Frenchy's cutlass. The doors to the parlor where the pit lay were slightly ajar. Whether it was my imagination or not, I smelled rotted meat and almost gagged. As I walked past a couple of women and their prospects, they grew quiet but for whispers. I paid little attention to them.

Billy Frieze stood with his back to the bar and a bottle in his hand. He nodded as I stepped up next to him and ordered a beer. The barkeep seemed to recognize me and hesitated, then slowly pulled a draft. The beer tasted as bad as the evening before, but I still drank it.

"Might fine buckskins, mate." Billy looked me up and down. "A natural fit, I'd say."

"All I have to wear." It was the first time I

140

had worn them since the bushwhacking. With my brother's knife showing at my belt and a beer in my belly, I was feeling more comfortable, and confident.

I ordered another beer. The room was still quiet, with most everyone talking low and staring at Billy and me.

"You know, mate, these folks think you're dead. A walking ghost, so they whisper. Are you?"

"If you stick me with a knife I'd bleed, like a bloody stuck pig," I answered, reminding him of the first sentence he ever said to me. I turned to face him. "Right?"

Billy chuckled. "Ah, a few days seems like a year now. As I recall, that evening you were going to stick me a couple a times, 'til I set the truth straight."

"Yes, the truth . . ." I sighed. Looking down, I saw that he had not changed his clothes, that dark bloodstains were spattered on his brown britches. "As I've come through the last couple a' days, knowin' the truth was the least of my worries."

Billy saw I noticed the blood and shrugged. "The truth is relative to who you're speaking with, where you happen to be standing at the time, and where you want to go. Right, mate?"

The tavern became noisier as more men

came in off the street. The women gradually turned their attention away from us, back to drinking and the evening's propositions.

"We leave for New Orleans tomorrow, at first light. On the *Diana,*" Billy stated. "First-class, paid for by Frenchy." He paused. "And as guests of his partner Fontenelle."

"Frenchy and Fontenelle, partners?" I asked, shocked by this new development. I knew Billy spoke the truth about other folks' comings and goings. It was everything in his personal life I suspected was a lie. "Partners in what?"

"Why, the American Fur Company, of course, along with Fitzpatrick."

"I don't understand, the company's owned by a man name of Aston, one of the richest bastards in the country. Everybody knows that."

"Not anymore, mate, John Jacob Astor is his name and sold it to Fontenelle and Fitzpatrick no more than a year ago, up at Fort Union." Billy lowered his voice. "Secret is, Frenchy's, shall I say, a silent partner in the deal."

I turned back to the barkeep and instead of ordering another beer, I asked for an empty glass. I motioned to Billy to fill it from his bottle, and then gulped the whiskey down. At that very moment, I wished badly to be back upriver with Anna, warm and safe from any controversy in which I had found myself involved. No matter that Rudy was dead and I was on my way to finding Baumgartner.

I pointed to my glass and Billy filled it to the brim. Raising it up, I indicated a toast. "To the new owners of the largest goddamn fur company in America and to their sinister circumstances therein, the bastards!" We both drained our glasses and slammed them on the bar. I was feeling the whiskey in my head and the beer in my gut.

"Why're you going to New Orleans, drummin' up business for yer brother in Bloody-Ole England? Ain't that what you said you're doin' on the river?" I stared at Billy, almost daring him to tell me another lie. I called the barkeep over, ordered another bottle of whiskey, and poured us both a drink.

"Mate, I'm going to help get your furs back and find Baumgartner."

"I don't need no help." I spat on the floor.

"Oh, no? You didn't need nor use my help finding Rudy, did you?" He raised an eyebrow then looked away toward the card tables under the stairs.

There was silence between us. As far as I

was concerned, our time for conversation was over. All there was for me to do was to keep drinking and be on that steamboat the next morning, bound for New Orleans.

A woman's moan became a wail, then a shriek. At the end of the bar stood Christine, her black eyes and bruised face shining by the light of the oil lamps.

"You, you fucking, murdering cock!"

I could not tell who she was screaming at, until her small fist slugged me in the side of the head, knocking me into Billy. With my back against the bar, she began pummeling me on the chest. To defend myself, I dropped the bottle I held, shattering it across the floor in front of us. I deflected her kick to my groin with a side step, grabbed both her wrists, and held them at her waist.

"Why are you hittin' me?" I shouted.

"She thinks you killed Rudy, mate," Billy calmly answered.

"How would you know? An' why in hell would she think that, *mate*?"

She tried twisting away but I held her tight. Most folks in the tavern were up on their feet and began to crowd around us, as they had the night before when she lay bleeding on the floor next to John Brigham.

Christine screamed, "Frenchy say you

144

come after Rudy, and he be dead now. He did nothing but cut you a little on your cheek and you kill him! You chop off his head!" With the broken nose and black eyes, her face contorted into some unnatural shadow.

She began wailing again and continued to kick. I struggled to hold her up and away from me. I did not want to hurt her.

"I didn't kill no one, least not here," I declared and then paused, still holding her away, her wild eyes staring up at me. I looked past her, to the crowd a few feet away, and saw a familiar face.

"I killed Rudy," Frenchy announced as folks edged away to let him through. It seemed the entire tavern inhaled a collective gasp, then silence. Broken glass crunched under Frenchy's boots as he stepped in front of me. Christine went limp, then shook her wrists free from my grasp and swung around to face him.

"You lie to me?" she whispered.

"Lie to you I don't, my sweet *Fille de Joie,* I merely don't tell the whole story."

"And what is the story? You murder Rudy Dupree, the only man who love me, Christine, your *Fille de Joie,* the whore!"

Frenchy caught her by the wrist as she tried to hit him and spun her back around, into his arms, tight, then leaned into her ear and whispered loud enough for all to hear. "Lied to me, your Rudy did. Lied to the only man who love him like his own son." He choked off the sentence and acted as if he wiped away a tear.

With both of them facing me, Christine glared down at the floor between us. Frenchy glanced up and gave me a quick wink. I tried stepping back but could go no further and stumbled on the bar's foot rail.

"Rudy Dupree, a man of certain talents, gifts if you may, will surely be missed." Frenchy drew Christine in closer and kissed her neck. "Always remember his love for you and my love for you both, *oui*?"

He slowly let go of her. She took a step toward me, snatched the knife from my belt, and spun back around, thrusting it at Frenchy. I grabbed her arm but she jerked away and stabbed at him again. He stepped backward, the crowd moving with him. Christine followed, blindly slashing. I pushed myself away from the bar, reached around, and grabbed her wrist as she thrust again, stopping the knife an inch from Frenchy's gut. He clamped his left hand around the blade and with his right hand peeled her thin fingers away from the handle. He handed me the knife, blood trickling from his palm. Christine cried out as he bent her wrist back, fingers cracking as he forced her to the floor. She lay curled in the spilt whiskey, blood, and broken bottle glass, softly moaning.

Gerard came through and broke the crowd up, sending the women back to their tables with their drinking customers and the gamblers back to their card games.

Frenchy disappeared.

Billy and I moved to the end of the bar and kept on drinking, not saying anything more to each other or to anyone else. I glanced over to Christine a couple of times. She lay on the floor for a long while sobbing, not moving but to nurse her hurt fingers and wipe tears from her eyes. I wished to say something, to lean down and somehow comfort her, but I knew I could do nothing. Eventually, one of the other women helped her off, I suppose, to a room somewhere upstairs.

The next morning, I sat with Billy out on the forward veranda, upper deck of the steamboat *Diana,* watching our departure. From the pilothouse one deck above us, a bell rang and rumbling began from deep within the bowels of the steamer. Another bell tolled. With a whoosh of steam and two loud whistles, we began moving backward and away from the landing of St. Louis, through the riffraff of riverboats and barges moored in the narrow, shallow channel.

I smelled cigar smoke and turned to Billy. He was looking up at a man standing behind us.

"Ah, what a thrill to be departing St. Louis on such a glorious fall morning. Don't you agree, Mr. Creed?"

I stood and moved my chair aside to face Fontenelle. Rather than the short coat and tie of summer and fall, he wore a winter coat and ascot, and of course, his beaver top hat. Before I could respond to his question, he handed me a folded piece of paper. With a look of contempt, he turned and strolled aft toward the slowly spinning paddlewheel. I sat back down and opened the paper.

Monsieur Zebadiah,
You owe me nothing. I owe you my life.
Frenchy

When *Diana* rounded the southern end of Blood Island, a man stood on shore, dressed much like a pirate. A young girl stood beside him holding his hand. The man gave a quick wave. The girl did not. Deep in my gut, I knew I would see them again.

We headed out to catch the main currents of the Mississippi and on to New Orleans. Two men were there I meant to kill.

CHAPTER 16

Natchez, Late September 1835

It was to be one game, Billy said. "Only one game and back to the boat, mate."

We were stopping in Natchez for wood and nothing more, is what I heard from one of the deckhands as I inquired why the *Diana* was slowing down. We would be off again by daybreak the next morning. The sun was setting beyond the flat, western shore of the Mississippi, the last of its light touching the tops of the Arkansas trees and golden smokestacks of the steamboat. On the eastern shore, beyond the half-dozen or so warehouses that stood a ways from the shore, lamps were being lit along the road leading up to the town of Natchez proper, which sat perched on a cream-colored bluff overlooking the wide river.

There was no wharf and I could not help but notice how vacant the shoreline seemed, not anything as busy as the landings in St.

Louis or Memphis. When I mentioned this to Billy, he nodded and said, "If left here unguarded, your cargo will likely be gone by midnight." He laughed, "Even then, you best be well armed."

I told him I thought it was not a good idea to go ashore, especially for only one game, that if he somehow missed the boat, he would be swimming his way on down to New Orleans.

"Then go with me," he said, ". . . an' keep me comp'ny. Together mate, we can surely make it back in time."

That was exactly what he said three days before, in Memphis, and I had chosen not to join him. He was late catching the boat the next morning by four hours. During that time, Fontenelle stopped me twice on the veranda to inquire about Billy's arrival. Once, he casually asked, "How will you find the men you look for in New Orleans without the help of your friend, Mr. Frieze?"

I had no answer for him, for I was shocked by his mention of my plan. Everyone it seemed knew my business. After St. Louis, I had not considered going to New Orleans alone, that Billy would accompany me to find Baumgartner and Brody. He seemed so well invested in his series of lies and half-truths not to follow me through to the end.

It was then I realized that without him, I might not finish what was started with the murder of my brother. I dared not tell anyone of my insecurities, certainly not Fontenelle. Hell, I could hardly admit them to myself.

That morning in Memphis, Billy was brought back to the boat by some local constable or sheriff, drunk and mumbling something about not deserving such fine treatment from the local Madame. He had lost all the money he carried and wore a knock on his head.

He complained all the way to Natchez about how badly his head hurt and there he was, again asking me to leave the boat with him. Though my answer left a bad feeling, I thought that going with Billy was better than him stepping off the boat alone and never returning.

Yet, I was hesitant to leave the relative safety and comfort of the *Diana,* especially after the dramatic events I experienced the week and half before in St. Louis. I would not say I had been driven to mental trauma, yet, once alone during the evenings, in my cabin, I found it hard to sleep. The sway of the boat did not help for I would have much rather had firm ground to lie on. I would wake several times during the night in a fit of sweat, feeling one wolverine tear at my leg, John Brigham, Frenchy, and Rudy standing above me laughing, and another purring wolverine circling from behind. My brother it seemed had left me alone to my nightmares.

The real comfort of the steamer came in the late afternoons, sitting on the veranda with Billy, drinking whiskey, watching the lush, hanging elms and willows sway in the breeze, their branches brushing the water. Tiny, silent hamlets floated by and nary a soul to greet us with a hello and a wave. Then from around some great bend, a bustling town would appear with ten or twelve steamboats and barges pulled along the shore. Our captain would always slow and blow his horn to greet his fellow captains. Everyone would respond in kind by blowing their horns mixed with a cacophony of whistles, whoops, and hollers. Day and night, the ever-widening Mississippi lay around us. Folks would say the river was more than a mile wide in some places, with its deep shoals, long, treacherous sandbars, and forest-covered islands; a water maze for our captain to navigate through. All the while, *Diana*'s paddles churned still, muddy water into a dirty whitewash left to disappear in her wake, leaving no trace of our journey.

I was not yet ready to depart this floating sanctuary, especially for an evening of card games with Billy Frieze, in a town known for the reckless behavior of its citizens.

The first mate checked his watch as we walked past. Fontenelle stood beside him. He glanced to Billy then looked right at me. "Bring him back safe," he said, smirking. "We would not want to leave either one of you behind, especially in a place such as this." We both stopped and acknowledged him with our nods and grins, as if we were schoolboys about to get into some mischief.

I followed Billy down the gangplank and onto the sand. There seemed only two businesses open and bustling, a cargo shed full of bales of cotton being readied for shipment and a locked pen with a dozen or so Negroes inside. A late-afternoon slave auction was going on in front, with a young man standing naked on a wood block. The dull, red scars across his back showed the world his plight. The auctioneer made bids, calling out the expected amount of money it took to buy the slave. The men who crowded around hollered numbers until the auctioneer yelled out *sold* to the highest bidder. We witnessed the young Negro man gathered in chains and hauled off to meet his new master. Billy stood glaring at the slaves in the pen. I nudged him forward and we kept walking.

"Goddamn savages," he whispered.

It was the first time I heard Billy say those words.

With a cool breeze floating off the river, we headed north on the sandy shoreline. Behind us lay the road up to the bluffs and to Natchez.

"Ain't goin' into town?" I asked.

"No, mate," Billy said, his demeanor changed. "Going up the coast a ways. Always a game or two where we're going. But we must hurry, running out of light to see the trail by, a mile or so and in." He stopped walking and stood still for a second, as if he were listening for something close, something on shore and not on the river. "I warn you, Zeb, there might be a wee bit of trouble ahead. Nothing too dangerous, mate."

I started spinning around in a slow circle with my coat slightly open. We were still on the sand below the bluffs and not too far away from the steamer. I had one knife and one pistol under my coat; I wished I had two of each and my brother's tomahawk.

"What's a wee bit a trouble, Billy?"

He shrugged and walked on. I followed,

155

with one hand on the pistol and the other on the knife. I wanted to believe he knew what he was doing and where to go.

We entered a dense forest washed with the sounds of crickets, frogs, and other strange noises, of southern birds and animals I was not familiar with nestling for the night. The full moon would not be up for another hour or so to see us through the trees. The dim twilight on the trail carried us forward. The air became sultrier the darker it became and I found myself sweating. Again, I wanted to be in my buckskins rather than the doctor's tight-fitting clothes and coat.

Within minutes, I heard many voices singing. I could not make out the words but the tune was familiar, as if I had heard it my whole life. Billy started humming to the song so I knew what I heard was real. I felt a chill when I realized it was the same tune Rudy whistled the day he pushed our keelboat off the sandbar.

From the trees, a black figure stepped in front of us. As I pulled my pistol, I heard the click of a flintlock from behind. "You boys lower whatever weapons ya have and carry on up the path. Harold will show yous which way to go." I felt a sharp nudge from the barrel of a rifle, pushing me forward into Billy.

"Expect ya come ta see the pastor?" Harold suggested. Neither of us answered. The man with the rifle pushed me again, harder. I swirled around with my pistol cocked and aimed it at his silhouetted head.

"I don't like to kill a man if I can't see his eyes, but if I'm to die out here in these woods, so will you," I stated casually.

"Now, now, gents!" Billy said. "We didn't come all the way from Ole St. Louie to find ourselves trouble in the dark forest. Why, we hear there is a card game that's waiting to be beat. Ain't that right, Zeb?"

"Yep." I held my pistol true.

"And I wager it's through those trees where all the singing's going on, right, Harold?"

"Right," Harold said.

"Well, then, I say lower them guns and, Harold, will you kindly guide us to the light?"

"I will not, else I get shot in the back," I stated.

Harold cleared his throat. "William, lower yer rifle now, we ain't out to kill nobody tonight, lest we have to. An' I reckon these fellers ain't too dangerous fer a walk in the woods."

As William lowered his rifle, I slowly lowered my pistol. Billy and I followed Harold on down the path. I was not nudged again.

The singing grew louder, and then fainter, then louder again as we crossed several paths, going left at the first one, left again, and then to the right. I lost count of the turns. Soon, through the trees, I saw the glow of fires lighting up the early-evening sky.

Harold passed between two camp tents and the singing stopped. The whole forest was quiet. He cleared his throat and announced, "Two lost souls a wanderin' through the woods at night ain't safe, I tell you. We brought 'em in for comfort, and a drink." He stepped aside; Billy and I walked into a large clearing. William stood next to Harold with his rifle by his side. Before us were three or four fire rings with several men seated around each one. At once, I noticed what a ragged bunch they were, with grease faces. Different kinds of hair, from sheared to long to nappy showed their true race. All of them were armed with at least three weapons each. Goats roasted on spits over a couple of the fires with hot coals sizzling from the dripping fat. Along the circular edge of the forest were scattered ten or twelve camp tents. At the far end of the clearing stood a brightly lit house, or church. Billy seemed to take in the scene with some sense of true excitement. I eased my pistol back into my belt. I was as anxious as I had been the first I stepped into Frenchy's Emporium. My experiences there warned me to be ready for anything to happen.

"Is the pastor in?" Billy hollered.

Murmurs wafted back to us from the fire rings. A man stepped out of the building's double doorway and onto the porch. "Who are ya?" he asked.

"I be Billy Frieze, and this be my mate Zebadiah Creed."

"And what er ya seeking, then?" The man slowly walked toward us.

"Why, sir, we want nothing more than a stout drink, a good whore, and a righteous game to fill the night out," Billy exclaimed.

The man stood in front of me, wearing very short black hair and a wire mustache. The smock he wore was white, except for a dark stain swashed across his chest, as if he had just wiped blood off the back of his hand. His breath smelled of river water. "What weapons do ya carry?" he asked.

"I carry none. My friend here, he's not as trusting and must be armed with something," Billy offered.

I stood eye to eye with the rogue, opening my coat to show him Frenchy's knife and the pistol at my belt. I did not offer them up. He reached for the knife. I snatched it up to his throat the same time I felt a sharp point poking into me. I glanced down to see him holding a blade at my belly. We held each other's fate for a few more seconds then he started laughing, his steel-blue eyes tearing up. The whole camp began to laugh, including Billy.

"Ya come here armed boy, ya best be ready to kill someone. Else ya might get killed yerself."

I eased Frenchy's knife back into my belt as my would-be assailant tucked his safely away. "Name's John Murrell," he said and bowed. "Welcome to the Devil's Punch Bowl, sir."

I offered my hand and we shook, his grip cold and hard. Thank you was all I could muster.

"Game starts with the moon risin' through them trees yonder way." He hooked a thumb over his right shoulder, east toward two huge oaks lit by firelight. "Come on in," he said and beckoned us to follow him up to the building. The closer we got, the more I realized that it was indeed a church.

I glanced at Billy. "Hell of a place for a card game."

"Aye, mate, I've heard the best," he said with a gleam in his eye, and we walked on into the church.

Outside, the singing resumed, as if the men were a choir, their voices raised in harmony to Heaven. Inside, the church was deathly quiet. I shuddered as I walked through the weather-beaten black doors. The few churches I had been in had many long rows of pews laid out across the floor to seat the congregation. This one lay bare except for a lone, round table in the center of the room with four plain wooden chairs circled around, the kind Fontenelle would sit in during dinner on the *Diana*. Eight pillars stood, holding up a broken, vaulted ceiling, with the only light coming from candles strung off hooks on each pillar. Dark patches of the evening sky shown through the holes in the ceiling. On the far back wall, behind the black pulpit, there hung a white cross. Or the clean, white paint where a cross once hung. The smell of mildew creep filled the sanctuary.

"Missionaries built it. Thought they would turn the savage beasts to Jesus. The savages were too smart fer that!" Murrell offered. "Look out yonder at them men singin'. My

clan. Why they're all mostly nigger an'
Injun, mixed blood. If ya get close 'nough
to smell 'em . . ." He whistled. A young,
dark-skinned girl joined us. "You can kill
'em, I suppose. 'Course, they sing my songs
beautiful, don't they, Mr. Creed?"

I did not know at all what the man was
speaking of, but I still answered. "Yes, sir,
they sing beautiful. I've heard this tune
before but don't know its name."

" 'Rock of Ages,' Mr. Creed. You heard a'
'Rock of Ages'?" Murrell's sunken eyes
shimmered.

"I sang that as a young boy sitting next to
me mom, with me brother," Billy said under
his breath.

Murrell kissed the girl hard on the lips
and smacked her backside, her plain white
dress no more than a mere slip to see
through. "Bring us some supper. Our friends
must be mighty hungry. And a new bottle."
He smiled as he watched her disappear back
into the shadows, beyond the candlelight.

The singing stopped in mid-verse, as if
something had struck down all the men at
once. Harold appeared at the double doors.
"The moon, sir. She's 'tween the trees."

"Ah, yes." Murrell approached the doors
with a slow, deliberate walk and stepped
outside. "William Wilkey," he stated loudly

to his men. "You have been called, son."

I grabbed Billy's coat, pulled him close, and whispered, "What have you brought us into, *mate*? This ain't just a goddamn card game!"

"Stay calm, Zeb, don't rile him up. He gets mighty testy when he gets riled up."

"So you know him, then? I thought you two were strangers. He seems not to know you." Murrell was still outside but I continued to whisper, though it was as if the walls of his church heard each of my words and felt my beginning panic. "We should leave, now. Somehow, knowin' you, you riled him up in the past an' I ain't stickin' 'round to find out how much!"

I let him go as Murrell walked back into the sanctuary. Following behind him was the man I almost shot in the forest. Outside, the singing recommenced with another hymn I was not familiar with.

"Gentlemen, this here is Mr. Wilkey. His friends call him William," Murrell announced, "ain't that right?" Wilkey glared at me and nodded, then lowered his head.

"He will join us at the round table." Murrell whistled and the girl appeared carrying a tray of roasted goat meat with wild onions and greens, a bottle and glasses. Where she came from, I did not know. I heard no door open or shut. She arranged the food and drink to seat four at the table, and disappeared back into the shadows beyond the pillars.

"Gentlemen, please sit," Murrell said and slumped into a chair with his back to the cross. The girl reappeared with an oil lamp and set it on a tall, narrow pedestal in the center of the table. Using a candle from the nearest pillar, she lit the lamp. Light shined down only on the table and chairs. Murrell's eyes glistened, as if he was about to cry. Yet, his face was calm, almost serene. I wondered why and how the blood ended up on his smock. He waved a hand, offering us each a seat. Wilkey hesitated then sat to his left, Billy to his right. I stood behind the chair opposite Murrell. I could not move. Even my skin screamed to get out of there and back to the boat. I was not so much afraid as I had a sense, a feeling. I did not want to die that night, in a crumbling church, in some god-awful place along the river called the Devil's Punch Bowl.

"Why do you hesitate?" Murrell's voice was mesmerizing, with his pitch raising or lowering to suit whomever he was speaking to.

"I ain't a card player," I said.

"Then why are you here?"

I gripped the back of the chair. I knew that if I lied, he would see right through me. "I'm here to get us back to our steamboat by daybreak."

Billy glanced sideways, at Murrell and then me. His face seemed to turn a shade red.

"An' why do ya think ya might have trouble with doin' that, sir?"

I could not help but look at Billy. Murrell's eyes followed mine.

"I don't know what to say, mate," Billy said with a sheepish grin. "I can be a bit excitable an' lose the track of time, if you get my meaning."

"Gentlemen, there ain't but one game this evenin'. No matter how long it goes to, is in God's hand . . ." Murrell chuckled, as if there was a joke to be found in his words. "An' I'm a itchin' to play that hand. Now, if you fellers . . ." he rose up from the table, ". . . snaked yer way through my woods an' still ain't got the gumption nor faith to play that hand with me, here at this table, well then . . ." He stood and pushed back his chair. The scrape across the wood floor echoed through the sanctuary. "Right, William?" he said, staring down at Wilkey.

"Right, sir." Wilkey's face turned as red as Billy's.

"An' if two fellers a wanderin' through my woods come stumblin' into camp with a rifle at their backs an' their intentions ain't true and known beforehand?"

I still stood behind the chair. "Weren't no rifle at our backs."

Murrell acted as if he was shocked. "So, either they walked in unnoticed, somehow knowin' their way, as if they'd been here before. Or . . ." He sat back down but did not pull his chair to the table. "This man," he nodded his head toward me, "give you the jump an' is now standin' in front of me with a loaded pistol at his belt, ready an' willin' to assassinate me for my crimes an' transgressions against society. William, do ya know what society is?"

"No, no, sir," Wilkey stuttered, "I reckon I don't."

"Society is all them folks we rile 'gainst to make a better world, a world fer us . . . fer us . . ." He stopped. "Ah, yes, the word comes to me now, cretins. You're a cretin against society, William."

Wilkey wore a confused look on his face.

"An' ya let these two society fellers waltz into camp as free an' easy as can be."

"I ain't no assassin," I stated.

"Then, sir, ya must be a cretin, like us?"

Murrell asked. All three men sat staring up at me.

"No, sir, I ain't."

"If ya ain't an assassin from society to come kill me, an' ya ain't a cretin like us, what are ya? Who are ya in God's eyes?"

Deep down, I felt I had answered this question before, in St. Louis, the night Frenchy asked who I was. The same night he so casually let go of the rope and sliced Rudy's head off.

I then remembered that, as I sat on the half-barrel with his black-eyed daughter staring at me, I never answered Frenchy's question.

"I am a savage, sir."

For the first time, I saw surprise on Murrell's face.

Wilkey slammed his hands on the table. "I shoulda shot yous!"

"Ya had not the will nor the chance, ya goddamn cretin," Murrell said softly and from under the table pulled two pistols, cocked one, and pointed it at me. The other pistol he cocked and *sha-boom,* shot Wilkey in the side of his head.

The concussion shook the foundation of the church and from somewhere above, I heard the panicked flutter of birds' wings.

Billy sat in shock, his mouth hung open

and his face a pale white. I stood staring down Murrell empty-handed, for I had no time or thought to pull my pistol. Wilkey's head lay face down in his food with blood filling the plate to the brim and spilling over onto the table. No one came rushing to the doors of the church. The young, dark-skinned girl did not emerge from the shadows. But for the hymn still being sung outside, a death silence surrounded us.

I slowly raised my arms above my head and pressed one hand across the other to keep them from shaking.

"What the fuck, *mate*!" Billy shouted.

"Didn't like his smell, damn sure didn't trust him. He allowed an assassin to come here. If I hadn't shot him when I did, ya woulda shot me, aye, Mr. Creed?"

"Hell man, we came here to play a bloody game of cards, not to kill anyone! Right, Zeb?" Billy could not sit still anymore and pushed back his chair with a scrape.

"Stay right there in yer seat, ya goddamn Brit. This here situation'll resolve itself very shortly an' you can go on 'bout yer business. I have no qualms with you."

Billy stopped squirming.

"Why'd ya kill him?" I asked, trying my best not to let my voice quiver.

"No. You ain't askin' the questions, I am.

First all, where were ya when he give ya the mark?"

"What mark?"

"Now, sir, don't play no games." Murrell sighed. "The cut on yer face, ain't nobody been cut by Rudy, an' lived, the son'a'bitch."

"Goddamn Rudy . . ." I said under my breath.

Murrell leaned nearer. "What you say?"

"I said the bastard's dead, long after he cut me."

"Hum, I heard rumors." He grinned slightly. "By your hand?"

"Yes," I said, without hesitating.

Billy shook his head fiercely and then glanced to Murrell, maybe to see if he had caught my lie.

"An' how?"

I smiled. "Cut the bastard's head clean off."

"Hum . . ." Murrell nodded. "With what, a sword?"

"I used a guillotine."

Billy was squirming again, swinging his attention to Murrell then back to me as we talked. Then, he simply sat on his hands, leaned over, and watched the blood seep through the cracks of the table.

"Where in hell, may I ask, did ya find a

169

guillotine?"

"My friend Frenchy, in St. Louis," I said, trying my best to look him right in the eye.

Murrell lowered his pistol slightly and nodded again. Then a gaping smile creased his face. The corners of his moustache stood straight across his narrow cheeks. At least two of his front teeth were missing.

"So . . ." He snickered. "Yer friends with Frenchy."

"Yes, sir, good friends."

"Well, sir, ain't that somethin', a friend a' Frenchy's." He raised his pistol and pointed it right at me. "An' you killed Rudy . . ." His eyes grew moist and he wiped them both with his sleeve. "So, Mr. Creed, I was beginnin' to trust you. Now I ask ya, how many more lies can there be this night 'fore I kill you, like I did ole William Wilkey here, huh?"

I tried to appear shocked that he would accuse me of not speaking the truth.

Murrell did not let me answer. "Ain't nobody friends with Frenchy. An' if ya ain't his friend, ya goddamn sure ain't using his guillotine to cut off Rudy Dupree's head."

The singing stopped. But for the rustle of a breeze through the openings in the ceiling and the restless night noise of the birds somewhere above our heads, it seemed the entire world was silent. I did not take my eyes off the mad man that sat across the table from me.

Murrell stared at Billy for a few long seconds. Then, as if lit by a spark, some sense of sudden recognition fell upon his face and his eyes teared up. "I know who you are, you're Billy Frieze!"

Billy sat back in his chair, looked at Murrell, to Wilkey and to the blood creeping its way to his side of the table.

"Don't believe we've ever met before this evening, mate," Billy stated with newfound confidence.

"Never met personal, but I know who you are." Murrell's face was nearly as pale as Billy's was. Again, he dropped the pistol a little, as if he were thinking what to do.

Footsteps sounded on the porch.

"You can go," Murrell said and waved his hand toward the doors.

Billy immediately stood and walked past me. I lowered my arms and started to move away from the table.

"Not you! Not Frenchy's friend!"

I froze, still facing Murrell. From behind me, I heard Billy step out to the porch and stop. Another man was waiting.

"Harold, make sure our new friend don't get lost in my woods." Murrell paused, and with the first hint of fear in his voice said, "An' Mr. Frieze, please give my best regards to your brother, will ya? An' any inconvenience I may have given you, sir, well, I do apologize." He sounded most sincere.

With the fade of his footsteps, Billy was gone.

Murrell squared back up to me, his pistol still aimed at my chest. "Now, sir, if you'd please, come on 'round to the table an' lay them weapons down, then have a seat. We'll talk awhile 'bout yer friend Frenchy 'an maybe find how true a savage ya really are." He grinned again and nodded at the plate sitting in front of me. "Honey, come get our new guest some hot food. After all this jawin' we've done, he's gotta be hungry."

The dark-skinned girl came out of the shadows and picked up the plate. She did not even glance at poor ole Wilkey, with his head face down in his food and his own blood.

Murrell leaned forward and gently placed his pistol on the table. "Now, Mr. Creed, go 'head an' tell me one more good lie, will ya?"

Under my breath, I cursed Billy Frieze, the bastard, and I cursed myself for never being much of a good, goddamn card player.

CHAPTER 17

Honey brought more food and I began to eat. I was not hungry but did not want to show Murrell any more disrespect than I had already shown him. Not because of any respect he deserved, I did not want to be shot for no good reason. The food was surprisingly good. Murrell ate from the same plate set in front of him before he shot Wilkey in the head. Though he seemed not to notice or care, there could have been bits of bone and brains mixed with the goat meat and vegetables. Watching him eat, I almost gagged on my own food.

One by one, Murrell's men entered the church to stand quietly in the shadows, their collective stench filling the sanctuary. In a few short minutes, the air became stiflingly hot and I found it hard to breathe. It was still the two of us at the table, and of course Wilkey. His blood had crept around the base of the lamp and along a wood seam to drip off the edge where Billy sat only a short while before. We ate in silence, as if we were sharing some sense of solemn solitude between us. I dare not show him any panic or true fear that I held inside myself.

With a wave of his hand, two of Murrell's men came, lifted Wilkey from the chair, and carried him away.

"Tomorrow morning, at dawn, we give him a proper burial. Do you know how we bury a man in the river? Would ya like ta know how we do that, sir?"

I slowly nodded.

"We fill their bellies full a rocks, take 'em to the middle, and slide 'em into the muddy water. They're gone in an instant."

"Do you say a prayer for them?" I asked.

He looked offended. "Well 'course we do! We're all God-fearin' men here. 'Specially Wilkey, he feared the most." A few of the men standing behind him chuckled and Murrell spun around with a quick-fired demon look in his eyes. "If any man not ever feared somethin' in their shit lives 'fore now, step on into the light."

Not even the rustle of birds' wings could be heard. The silence hurt my ears. No one stepped forward.

Murrell slowly turned back to me. "Told ya, ain't nothin' but cretins." He took a finger, wiped the plate clean, and stuck it in his mouth. He sucked off the last of the food. "Now, Mr. Creed, we're goin' to play a game. Ya don't like card games, ya might like this one. I ask ya three questions. Two ya tell the truth, an' one ya lie. I get to guess which is which. If I guess right, I tie you to that chair ya sittin' in an' have my men throw ya in the river, right next to poor Wilkey. Except you ain't sinkin', you float away alive. 'Course 'til that chair turns upside down. An' well then, lest ya can breathe old muddy water . . ."

"How will you know I speak the truth?"

He laughed with almost a whistle sound, showing again the gap where his teeth used to be. "Mr. Creed, you will tell me when ya speak the truth an' when ya lie." With a flick of a finger, he pointed to the untouched bottle. "Honey, come here an' pour our new friend a drink, will ya?"

The girl again came from the shadows, poured the liquor into a glass, and gently placed it in front of me. For the first time we met eye to eye. Her glance was quick, with a smile even quicker.

"Drink up, now," Murrell said.

"Ain't thirsty."

"Don't much care, drink up I said." He picked up the pistol and stared at me from across the table.

If I were to stand, pick up my weapons, and simply walk away, I might have made it to the double doors, but not beyond. Instead, I lifted the glass to my lips and drank.

"All of it," he said.

I drank it and she poured me another. I did not know what the smooth liquor was; it tasted like berries but was not wine. I liked it and drank the second glass down.

"Why are ya goin' to New Orleans?"

"Kill two men."

"Who?"

"Is that your second question?" I gave him a slight smile.

"Still part a' the first." He looked away, into the shadows. Again, a couple of his men chuckled. He did not react and turned back to me for my answer.

"Don't seem fair," I said.

"Fair's what I say's fair."

I did not hesitate. "Man named Baumgartner and Benjamin Brody."

My answer set off his clan to murmuring among themselves. He could not conceal his surprise. He leaned forward and stroked his pistol. "Hmmm . . ." was all he said for a few long seconds.

"Why in hell are you goin' to kill those two?" he asked as if he knew them both.

"Because one killed my brother an' the other put him up to it."

Murrell continued to stroke the pistol. Though it lay on the table, it was aimed right at me.

"The big man in New Orleans an' his second? Now, sir, I ain't no society, an' the more you an' I talk, more I realize you ain't, either. So you goin' ta waltz right on down there an' kill 'em both?"

"That's your third question?"

He slammed the butt end of the pistol down on the table. "No, damn you!"

I cracked a smile, then calmly said, "My intentions are to find them both unattended and put a ball 'tween their eyes, just like Baumgartner shot my brother, right 'tween the eyes."

Murrell laughed again. "Just like that?"

"Just like that. Then I'm gonna scalp 'em both."

Without a pause, he asked, "So . . . that's how ya found Rudy, just like that?"

"Scalped? No, sir, first I laid eyes on him in St. Louis he had his scalp, was strapped to the guillotine. Wasn't a few minutes later, he lost his whole head."

"No, no, how'd ya find where he was in St. Louie? Ya didn't just stumble on him, did ya?"

"Oh, no, sir, Frenchy led me to his special sittin' room where he kept all his weapons, is where I found Rudy."

The briefest look of jealousy crossed Murrell's face. "I've only heard of such a place," he said, more to himself. "By your hand?"

"No, sir, Frenchy let go the rope."

He sat back in his chair and looked straight up to the darkness of the sanctuary's broken ceiling. When he lowered his eyes back to me, they glistened. "How'd he cut'cha?"

"Who?"

"Rudy, goddamn it!" he shouted.

"After I shot Baumgartner's hat off his head, Rudy came at me, cut my cheek, an' was to run me through. Baumgartner stopped him."

"Hmmm . . . why'd he stop him, do ya think?" Murrell's tone softened, as if he was surprised that Baumgartner would do such a thing as save another man from getting his throat cut.

"After Jeffery gettin' his face split open by my brother's tomahawk an' us both gettin' shot, I guess it didn't much matter, we was goin' to die anyway." The drink was getting to me for I felt sad, for the way I lost Jonathan and for the whole damn situation I found myself in.

Murrell again looked confused. "So, they left ya to die?"

"Yes, sir, 'course after shootin' a ball through my brother's head, kinda like you done with Wilkey here, an' Rudy knockin' me in the head with my brother's tomahawk, the same one that killed Jeffery."

"Where'd all this take place, St. Louie?"

"No, sir, way up near Arrow Rock, on the Missouri."

"What the hell were ya doin' way up there?"

"That's 'bout fifteen goddamn questions, should we stop an' count the lies?"

Without hesitating, he picked up the pistol and pointed it at me. "Ya keep talkin', sir, an' I'll let ya know when we start countin'."

"We was bringin' our beaver pelts to market."

"From Rendezvous? Why not sell 'em to the fur comp'ny?"

I drained my glass and raised it for more liquor. The girl again came from the shadows and filled the glass to the brim. I could hear the restless feet of Murrell's men surrounding us, though I could not see their faces. I felt that our conversation was about to end.

"Thought we'd get a better deal on our own," I said.

"Whew wee! You went against them bastards?"

"Yep."

"An' Rudy an' that cocksucker Baumgartner came after an stole all yer furs, didn't
they?"

"Yep."

Murrell sat in silence for a few long
seconds with a look of surprise, then amuse-
ment. He smiled and slapped his hand
down on the table. "Rudy workin' fer the
fur comp'ny, I'll be a son-bitch! Hell, man,
he deserved to die, the . . . the . . . the
fuckin' traitor."

He leaned forward and a shadow fell
across half his face. "An' what of yer friend
Frenchy, aye? What of his place in this . . .
mess with Rudy?"

I shrugged and took another drink. "Don't
know, 'cept they seemed to know each
other. Frenchy mentioned goin' back to
Terre Bonne. Don't know what or where
that is. Do you?" The drink was making me
bold.

"Barataria . . ." he simply said.

The sanctuary began to swirl around me.
I set the glass down and took hold of both
arms of the chair.

Murrell drummed his fingers on the table.
"Sir, ya appear to be a bit wrung out. Hold

together a while more, we ain't done yet."

"Why's Rudy so important to ya?" I slurred.

Without hesitation, Murrell answered, "He was once one of us, long time ago." His eyes swelled, as if he would cry.

"Oh . . ." was all I could say.

He motioned me to lean across the table, to get closer to him. With his eyes shining, the half-shadow on his face made him appear to be quite mad. "Frenchy killed Rudy same reason I killed Wilkey," he whispered.

"An' why is that?" I whispered back.

He glanced around, to his men standing beyond the candlelight and turned back to me. "Secrets, Mr. Creed, they died full a secrets."

My confusion must have shown on my face.

"They're all in league with one 'nother," he exclaimed. "Baumgartner an' Rudy, Frenchy an' the goddamn fur comp'ny. They're all in cahoots, don't ya see?"

Billy was right, he must've been, the son-of-a-bitch! Thinking back to what he claimed about Frenchy becoming a silent owner in the American Fur Company. I did not want to believe it to be true.

"Thoughtless violence, sir," I stated aloud.

Murrell gave me a look of disbelief and

181

then pity. "Ain't no such thing," he said. Then, "I can't help ya to understand anymore'n I have helped ya already." He seemed frustrated that I did not agree with his sense of things.

"Can I go now? I answered yer goddamn questions, more than three to be sure an' I don't want to miss my boat to New Orleans." In my mind, I had enough and was already preparing myself to walk my way through the woods by moonlight, back to my cabin and to bed.

"Oh, no, we ain't done yet. I have one more question, probably the most important, more personal."

I heard groans from the shadows, as if his men were ready for something a little more exciting than talk.

"What makes ya think yer a savage?" He smiled. "Now, don't lie, I'll catch ya."

I thought for a second and with a sense of clarity, I said, "Let me tell you a story."

"You go right ahead," Murrell said, crossing his arms.

"Well, sir, we was way up near Pierre's hole, back earlier in the year, durin' spring. My brother an' me. We weren't so much trappin' our beaver as usin' nets. The way we was shown."

"Showed by who?"

"Our folks, our kin. From early on, we was raised by Lakota."

Murrell whistled again, smiled, and slapped his hand on the table. "I knew there was somethin' 'bout you! Hell, are ya one a them sun dance warriors?"

"Yes, sir, I am."

"Show me."

I slowly lifted up my shirt. The scars on my chest seemed to shine in the lamp light.

"I'll be goddamned! How long did ya hang for?"

I pulled me shirt down and took another long drink. "Three days an' nights."

"Whew weee . . . hangin' from the sky." He turned around to face the shadows and his men. "Now there's somethin' to live up to!" No one responded.

He turned back, shaking his head, and waved for me to continue.

"My brother an' me, we came up Spindly Creek to check our nets. As soon as we got close, we smelled smoke. We loaded our rifles an' crept close to a camp set a ways off the shoreline. There were two of them, same as us. It was early afternoon an' we musta spooked 'em. Or since they were stealin' our beaver, they knew to be ready for us. Before we could holler who we were, one of 'em stood an' took a shot at us. Well, my brother Jonathan wasn't too keen on getting' shot at, especially when the one doin' the shootin' was stealin' our beaver. He took aim and shot the man down."

Murrell was grinning like a coon. "I like who yer brother is! He don't hesitate, now does he?"

"Was sir, I told you, he's dead."

"Well shit, I'm sorry. Was, I like who he was!"

My glass was empty so I reached for the bottle. It was then I realized that Murrell had not drunk a drop of the liquor. I was getting woozy again but could not stop myself from filling my glass.

"When we reached their camp, the one man lay dying on the ground. The other thief was nowhere to be seen. Jonathan placed the butt end of his rifle onto the man's gut wound and kindly asked where his partner had run off to. He didn't answer. Couldn't 'cause he died right then, there in his own camp."

"That ain't nothin'. Hell, he deserved to die, the goddamn thief." He leaned over the table again. "So what makes you more savage then me?"

I leaned in and met him eye to eye. "I ain't finished with my story yet. We knew the other fella couldn't be far, so went lookin' for him. We searched an' searched an' nothin'. We was standin' on the shore of the creek, overlookin' the beaver lodge, when we heard somethin' like a stick break. Then the whole damn lodge shook, like there was somethin' inside. Now, we knew it wasn't no beaver, they had already been skinned an' stretched out as plews an' laid out to dry back at their camp. I went an' got me a piece a' burnin' wood an' some dried brush an' climbed down on the lodge. I lit the brush an' dropped it into the air hole on top figurin' I'll smoke the bastard out." I paused and lowered my head. I could not look Murrell in the eye any longer. "Hell, I didn't know the whole goddamn lodge would catch fire as quick as it did, in springtime, with the snowmelt an' all."

The sanctuary was quiet. I thought his men to be more restless for standing still almost an hour, but not a boot scuffed the floor.

"So, how'd ya know he was in there?"

"We heard his screamin'."

"Hmmm . . ." Murrell sat still and stared at me.

The inside of the church went to swirling again and the men in the shadows began to file out, except for two. They stayed to throw a rope around my upper arms and chest. I struggled but was too drunk to fight them. They left me tied to the chair. Murrell continued to sit across the table and stare at me.

"You, sir, are indeed a savage burnin' that man alive." He did not give up his stare. "Yet, you did lie to me, an' I can't have that."

"When the hell did I lie, ever thing I said was true!"

"Not ever thing," he said, mocking me. "Ya claimed to be friends with Frenchy. Well, ain't nobody friends with him."

He stood, leaned over the table one last time, and blew the lamp out.

Chapter 18

The church is new and filled with light, not sunlight, another kind that only shines in dreams. The pews line up facing front and are filled with folks, a mix of Negroes, Indians, and whites, folks that seem both familiar and strange at the same time. The table and my chair sit right in the middle of the church, as if the pews had been cut around. Murrell is at the pulpit preaching, though I do not hear a word, for behind him, the cross on the wall is black, a deep shadow hung against pure white paint, and all I can think of is how a shadow can hang there on a wall. The young girl stands by my side, smiling down at me, holding my hand. She gives a tug and slowly unbuttons my britches, pulls them down a ways and with her plain dress lifted up, straddles me. I know this is wrong and try to stop her but with my arms tied to the chair, I cannot resist. I close my eyes and let her heat seep into my skin. I have not felt such pleasure since my wedding night years before, in my own teepee, with my wife. I strain the ropes to reach out and hold her. All I can do is caress her thighs with my hands as she rises up and thrusts down. Murrell stops preaching and all the congregation is watching. The first I recognize is William Wilkey. Sitting next to him is the man I burned alive in the beaver lodge. Behind him sits my brother. On the other side of Jonathan sits Rudy. I do not care if they watch us. We finish and I am drained, yet I feel the most fearless that I have ever felt. She lets her thin dress fall back into place and with a dirty finger brushes my cheek and scar. A scream pierces the silence, a scream I have heard before, buried deep beneath burning sticks and mud. He stares at me, the man I burned up. He stares at me and screams . . .

I woke to the flapping of birds' wings above me. I looked up and saw small sparrows swoop down from the rafters and catch tiny morning moths fluttering about in the beginning light of dawn. I was still tied to a chair in the middle of an empty sanctuary, sitting next to a round table covered with dried blood. Outside, the camp of men was waking and soon I knew Murrell would be returning. I glanced down to my lap. I was not surprised to see my britches unbuttoned. I swept the sanctuary looking for the girl. Past the pillars, with the shadows gone, there was nothing more than broken pews strewn along the walls. A single door led into a smaller room where she must have come back and forth through the darkness. I wanted to see her. I strained against the rope and could not budge it. The only hope I had was that both my arms below the elbow were free and they had not tied my feet. I buttoned my britches back up.

I did not remember much from the night before, except Billy leaving, drinking the liquor, and telling stories to keep myself from being killed by a mad man. It seemed even the telling of true tales could not save me. I wondered what Billy was doing, the bastard. Was he up on the veranda desperately awaiting my return or was he laughing with Fontenelle about my impending demise? No matter, I was still alive and I could not concern myself with what went on with him. Though I was sad to miss the *Diana*'s departure, for I had become rather fond of being onboard the smelly old steamboat.

I recognized Harold's footsteps on the

porch and on into the church. From behind, he leaned down to my ear and said, "If he slits yer throat I'll do nothin' but laugh. I wanted to leave yer friend in them woods an' let the demons get him." He stepped back, as if he was listening for something, or someone. "One day, that Brit'll get his. Today, you'll get yours. William was my friend."

"Where's the girl?" I asked.

"What girl? Ain't no girl here."

Boots sounded on the steps and Harold was quiet. I knew it was Murrell among others.

"Well, sir, no time to hesitate. We're off to our most sacred place on the river," he stated. "Boys, keep him tied to that chair. Harold, give 'em a hand, will ya?"

Harold and a dark-skinned man with stick hair picked me up, one at each arm, and carried me out the double doors into the sunshine. A rather solemn procession, with Wilkey's wrapped body raised above everyone's heads, entered the forest to the north. We followed toward the end with Murrell bringing up the rear. We snaked our way through the trees, with some men humming the same hymn they sang the evening before. For some odd reason, I was soothed by their voices.

We broke through the trees out to what seemed to be a flat, open field, except for the river expanding for a mile beyond where the earth ended. Most of Murrell's clan stood in a half-circle facing the water. As we got closer to the edge, I saw that we were on a bluff looking south toward Natchez by a couple of miles. I was set down next to Wilkey's body facing the trees. From downriver, a whistle blew twice then a third time. Murrell motioned for Harold to turn me around. I could see that the *Diana* was still at the waterfront. With one more whistle blown, the paddles began to move and the steamboat crept backward into the river. Within a minute or so, she was well on her way to New Orleans.

"Lookin' like ya missed yer boat," Murrell said. He made a motion and Harold turned me around again to face the forest. The back legs of the chair were right at the edge.

I was beyond angry, or afraid. If I was to die there, on that bluff, so be it. The sun was shining with a nice wind blowing and I would somehow take at least one of those men with me to my death.

Murrell stood with his head down, as if in prayer. Wilkey's body lay at his feet. Someone had unwrapped it, cut the belly open, and filled it full of hand-sized stones. A rope and a piece of canvas kept the stones from falling out.

"We are gathered here to consummate our dear friend, William Wilkey, back to the all-mighty river from whence he came." He paused for several long seconds. "Can I hear amen?"

All of his clan answered back with a loud *Amen*. No one missed a beat. Two Negroes dressed in coyote skins picked the body up and with a couple of good swings, tossed it off the bluff. From somewhere below, there came a heart-wrenching splash.

Murrell turned back to me. At his belt, he carried Frenchy's knife. He leaned in close and whispered, "Been nice knowin' ya."

I snatched the knife, stood up to look into his watery eyes, pressed the tip of the blade to his belly, and said, "My friend Frenchy gave this to me." I pushed myself backward off the edge of the bluff. The last I saw of John Murrell was his toothless smile as he watched me fall.

The chair shattered when I hit the water thirty feet down. By the time I cut off the rope, the swift current had carried me on toward Natchez by a quarter mile. I dared not stop there, for I did not want to be captured again. Murrell would certainly not let me go a second time.

Past the landing, by an hour in the water, I came upon a timber barge the length of three steamboats, similar to the one John Brigham must have taken all the way from Minnesota to St. Louis. As I hollered to be fished out of the water, I thought, *Maybe there'd be one more man needs killin' when I get to New Orleans.*

CHAPTER 19

New Orleans, October 1835
"You get caught up in them mountains. It's a long time 'tween summers."

Blue smoke curled up from an ember burning in the pipe. She breathed in, and then asked, "Why do you go there, *Monsieur* Zebadiah?"

I did not answer.

Her name was Sophie le Roux, a French woman with a bit of Indian and Negro in her. But for lines of age and opium-stained lips, she was still sumptuously beautiful. Her eyes shined black diamonds. I was fortunate to be in her favor, for she was the richest Madame in New Orleans.

She brushed back a wisp of graying black hair and closed her eyes. "So, my Mountain Man, what brings you back to New Orleans and to me?"

Wind and rain blew against a small, cracked window beside a plain four-post bed. Lit only by a single oil lamp, her room was Spartan compared to that of other women of her sort. Next to the door, a porcelain water bowl, pitcher, and matching chamber pot lay carelessly pushed against the wall. On a low square table sat a dusty bottle of cognac with two crystal glasses and a gold and copper water pipe. Between our chairs, burning embers glowed in a cast-iron kettle. Of course, this was her sleeping room, not her entertaining room.

"You are familiar with a certain Englishman I seek . . ."

She opened her eyes. "I am familiar with many Englishmen. A few I am fond of, most I am not. Why do you seek this man?"

I picked up my glass. "He owes me."

Sophie took a long draw from her pipe. Smoke seeped from her nose as she spoke. "We do not leave this life owing no one. I suspect he owes you more than money and there is to be a fight?" She paused. Another draw sent her coughing. She recovered, but with a subtle look of embarrassment. Then, "A man will only fight over a woman, an insult, or revenge. Which is it for you, *Monsieur* Zebadiah?"

I stood, walked to the window, and stared down at a dark, muddy street and the black swamp beyond. For an instant, I thought I saw a flicker of light, perhaps a boat lantern rapidly hidden or extinguished, or perhaps only my imagination.

I turned back to her. "An insult, thievery, and spilt blood."

"Your Englishman's name is?"

"Benjamin Brody."

"Ah, *Monsieur* Brody . . ." she whispered. Her black eyes shone through blue smoke.

"You have bathed and are now wearing a clean shirt, new britches, and boots. My women have taken good care of you, *oui*? You have eaten and drunk well with intimate conversation?" She paused and for the first time smiled. "And your wounds are healed?"

"My wounds?" Of the two women who helped me, I wondered who told her of my shoulder and faded bruises on my chest.

"Oh, *cherie,* my girls tell their Madame everything. They did question how the splinters ended up in your . . . your . . ."

"I fell backward in a wood chair an' smashed it," was all I said.

She stood and stretched. Reaching up, her long, thin fingers seemed to touch the ceiling. She closed her eyes again and began to dance, her ample hips swaying back and forth. The rain had slowed to a drizzle, and but for the whoosh of her petticoat, the room was silent. I sat down on the bed and finished my drink. I could hear her breathing, almost humming. A waltz to go with her dance, a ghost melody she seemed to only half recollect. With her eyes still closed, she unhooked the top of her dress.

"You will stay the night with me, yes, *Monsieur* Zebadiah? Tomorrow we shall discuss how to accommodate you further with this Englishman Brody." A second hook came loose by her fingers. "One more question, then no more." A third hook popped loose. "I ask again, why you go to the mountain when everything is here in this room?"

She finished unhooking the dress, pulled it up over her head, and carelessly dropped it to the floor. She slipped out of her petticoat and undergarments. Glistening by oil lamp, she stood naked before me.

Under her spell, I could not think to answer properly.

CHAPTER 20

Fingers touch my bare back. I turn. She falls into my arms and we kiss, deep, a familiar kiss, yet new, with experience. We lay together on the hay-stuffed mattress, for the first time, making strong love, breathing life into each other. Exquisite quivers of pleasure send through us. Afterward, she cries softly. We stand, embrace, naked at the open window. A light breeze flutters the curtains; goose bumps rise up on our skin. With a smile, she closes her blue eyes, lays her head against my chest, and sighs. I gaze out the window, to the black swamp across the muddy, New Orleans street, and I stroke Anna's curly blonde hair.

Sophie left me the next morning with a breakfast of Tourtiere pie, Johnnycake, scrambled eggs, ham and coffee. I did not leave a crumb. Standing by the open window, I felt morning sunshine for the first time since leaving St. Louis two weeks earlier.

Her house faced Liberty Street. Not a main thoroughfare by any means, but busy with fleet and cargo wagons carrying goods to the east market or on south to the Mississippi. It seemed white slave owners and freed men of color strolled side by side along the boardwalk beside the muddy street.

An inlet, more a finger of the great swamp, lay across from the house. A wharf ran along the shore where two boatmen unloaded several bundles wrapped in hemp off a small river barge then threw them into a wagon to be driven away. One of the men looked up to the house and I backed away from the window.

I lay down on the bed and waited on Sophie's return.

Jonathan and I had been to New Orleans two years before, so I was no stranger to the city. The clamor and noise I did not find too intimidating, but the filth, smell, and confines were unsuited for one so used to clear air, few folks, and open land. I also knew I had to be more careful of my actions. New Orleans had the law and St. Louis did not.

I woke with a start to thunder and the stale smell of mold. It was early twilight and Sophie sat cutting slices of marbled cheese and an apple. An open bottle of red wine and two glasses were on the table. She noticed I was awake and smiled.

"Before entering the room I heard you snoring," she sighed. "Your journey has been long and tiring, no?"

I rubbed my eyes and looked out the window. It was raining again. As I sat up, Sophie handed me a slice of the cheese on some bread and a piece of apple. I took one bite of the cheese and winced. She laughed then motioned to bite into the apple. The crisp sweetness of the fruit cut some of the foul taste.

"Ah, Zebadiah, you do not like my *bleu* cheese? We leave it in the cupboard in the kitchen until ripe. Here, a little wine to wash out the taste." She poured me half a glass with another slice of apple. I leaned toward her. She did not bend to kiss me nor did she offer any other kind of intimacy.

"So, tell me of your brother's death . . ." she said casually.

"And how do you know of him?"

"As fast as a steamboat, word travels downstream, *Monsieur* Creed. Don't you know? Besides, he is not here with you."

Her eyes narrowed. "Now, tell me a story of your brother, and St. Louis."

I looked away again to the open window and the rain clouds beyond. I resented being in her charge but could not yet show my true feelings.

Turning back, I began to tell my story as I had with Frenchy, this time with some discretion.

I told her of the two men who bushwhacked us, with little detail of Dr. Keynes and his daughter, other than them bringing me back from death. St. Louis was still fresh in my mind and I hesitated when she asked more about Frenchy and his emporium. I did not tell of his daughter Sapphire and her extra senses nor did I go into detail about the pit and the way Rudy was killed. She did not react surprised through much of the story, including my telling of Jonathan's murder. When I mentioned Billy Frieze, her eyes lit up.

"This man I know, how did you meet?"

"On the steamer between Boonville and St. Louis, he came to my cabin one evening and introduced himself, sayin' he may know the whereabouts of the murderin' thieves."

"And how did he know you were searching for them?"

"A man named Fontenelle gave me up."

I did not lie so much as not tell her of my own indiscretions with one of the new owners of the American Fur Company.

"He is downstairs now."

"Fontenelle?"

"No, my *cherie, Monsieur* Frieze."

My face burned. I had not seen him since Natchez five days before. "And how did he come to be in your establishment this evening?" I did not disguise my anger.

Sophie smiled and swiped away wisps of graying black hair from her eyes. "I invited him."

"You know this scoundrel Billy Frieze well enough to have him here on my behalf?"

"Certainly you presume he's here because of you. However, on my own accord do I have business with *Monsieur* Frieze." She paused, taking a drink of her wine. "To be frank with you, Zebadiah, I am quite fond of him . . ." She reached over and stroked my cheek. "Almost as fond as I am of you."

Before she could touch me again, I stood and turned my back on her to stare out the window. Evening carriages lined the street below as men in top hats and umbrellas took their turns entering the bordello. Laughter drifted up from the parlor.

The rain had not let up.

"Shouldn't you be leaving now, to go

downstairs?"

"Ah *cherie,* of all New Orleans I have a dozen of the finest young ladies, ages fourteen to twenty-three, lining up to greet my guests. They do not need an old woman to do their picking and choosing."

From behind, I felt her arms wrap tight around my waist. Her fingers smelled of *bleu* cheese. With her head laid against my back, she whispered, "My Juliette will bring you dinner and suitable clothes. When you are ready, come down. There will be a man to speak with, to help you decide how to best approach *Monsieur* Brody and, how you say his name, *Baumgartner?*"

Sophie let go, crossed the room, and opened the door.

"Does it always rain here?" I asked, still staring out the window.

"*Oui,* Zebadiah, always."

I turned to find her standing in the doorway.

"Last evening, as you lay asleep in my arms, you called out to another woman . . ." Her black eyes bore into me. "She must be lovely."

Without waiting for my response, Sophie slowly closed the door behind her.

CHAPTER 21

Juliette brought me supper and more wine. She was a young woman of modest dress, maybe seventeen or eighteen, with sandy-colored hair. Her golden-brown eyes sparkled. She smiled and said nothing as she left the room. A moment later, she returned with a clean shirt, evening coat with vest, suspenders, and trousers, and laid them on the bed. As I dressed, she adjusted the suspenders and helped with my boots and coat, all the while in silence. She pointed at the food and made a gesture to eat, then nodded toward the door, as if to remind me that I was expected downstairs. Juliette left again, with not a word spoken between us.

I made my way down the back passage from Sophie's room to the second floor. There I paused, as I had two years before, to take in a full view as the grandest staircase I had ever walked down opened to the crowded parlor below. The handrails and spiral columns were the cream color of mother's milk, with black oak steps so shiny I thought I might slip and fall. Against the landing wall, purple velvet drapes hung from the ceiling along each side of a rectangular stained-glass window. The design depicted an open door with the moon shining beyond, a door within a window. I stood absently caressing the cool stone handrail. Though Sophie had said she would introduce me as a close friend from St. Louis, I was not sure if I was up for another charade such as the one attempted on the steamboat *Diana.* I slowly descended the stairs, thinking her establishment was nothing at all like Frenchy's Emporium. After all, this was the city of New Orleans, not the frontier town of St. Louis. What all whorehouses had in common, however, were men with money and their insatiable appetites for painted ladies. With that thought in mind, I entered the fray.

Sophie met me at the bottom step. With her hair pulled up, she looked splendid wearing a dress the color of a yellow rose. Her bosom shone brilliantly by candlelight.

"Ah, my love, you are so young and handsome," she gushed. "You must help me make the old men jealous. Come, and say hello to everyone." I bristled at this but allowed her to take my arm. She sashayed her way through her guests and ladies, introducing me to anyone who had not already disappeared or was busy feigning privacy on a couch. Most of the men looked important, with their titles only alluded to, as if to speak aloud that one was a sheriff or a prominent council member might somehow shame their experience. Or take away some of the excitement of it.

Sophie knew them all well.

The only voice I recognized above the din was Billy's and my face burned. Before I saw him, I heard his laugh and knew he was already drinking. I hesitated as Sophie pulled me through an open arch, under the stairs, and into a garden.

"Hello, mate!" Billy shouted. "Goddamn, where have you been, Zeb?"

I was not shocked at seeing him, nor the tall black-skinned man. It was the woman standing between them I had my eyes on, dressed in tight pink silk from head to toe. She smiled, then covered her mouth, as if ashamed. Slowly lowering her hand, her red lips quivered with a slight grin. She glanced away and then back to me, her slanted green eyes matching exquisitely with her almond face. I immediately thought Lakota, yet I had never seen a Lakota woman so beautiful.

Sophie poked me in the ribs. "Zebadiah, you drop your jaw."

"Looks like you seen a ghost, mate," Billy said.

Sophie looked to Billy, then to the Negro. "*Monsieur,* for my guest's behavior, I am sorry. I presume he has not seen one so . . ." she paused for a quick glance to the other woman, "exotic."

I ignored Billy and stuck my hand out. "I'm sorry, it's just that . . ."

The gentleman shook my hand. "You have never seen Chinese?" He turned to the woman and smiled. "I will agree with your reaction, for it was mine also when first we met." He held on to my hand. "Let me introduce myself, my name is Olgens Pierre."

"Name's Zebadiah Creed," I said and let go. I could not remember ever shaking a Negro man's hand before. It was not at all rough like I expected, and he wore rings on his fingers. I had never seen a man dressed so fanciful, his suit cut from the finest cloth and of the latest style. His top hat was made of prime beaver pelts with a colorful feather plume. Though he, Billy, and the Chinese woman stood at the entrance to the garden rather than with the white folk in the main parlor, he was certainly a man of wealth.

"Mr. Pierre might help us with our problem, mate."

I glared at Billy. "What problem is that, *mate*?"

"Zeb, you know, with Baumgartner and . . ." He took a drink then looked around, as if to make sure no one else was interested in hearing our conversation. "Brody?"

"Billy, it ain't your goddamn problem." Wanting to spit, I swallowed what I really wanted to say to him.

Sophie grabbed my hand and forced me to step toward Billy. "Ah *cherie,* into the garden you both go and set this disagreement right."

She led us both up a short walk lit by torches, through roses and orchids, to a small empty bandstand. As soon as the three of us were sheltered, it began to rain again.

"The two of you have much in common, far more than me." Sophie giggled, like one of her young girls might giggle. "I leave you to solve your differences."

She stepped off into the rain and ran hard, trying not to get her lovely dress too wet, back to the archway where Pierre and his Chinese woman still stood.

Billy leaned against the rail, pulled a bottle from his belt, and took a swig. Even with the overwhelming scent of roses and wet dirt, I could smell that it was good whiskey. He offered me a drink. This reminded me of our first meeting, in my cabin on the *Diana,* when Billy told me he knew of Baumgartner and Brody. The difference being standing in a garden with rain pouring down around us, I held no knife as I had then, to run him through. I was angry at what he did in Natchez, but deep down, not enough to kill him.

"You left me," I said calmly.

"I had to, mate, he woulda hurt me, hurt me bad."

I nodded in agreement, for the man I was left with in the church sanctuary was a mad man. He might not have hurt Billy, no one would ever know. Hell, he shot his own man for no good reason other than to prove a point.

"After missin' the steamer, I took a timber barge on down the river, was at the mercy of the crew. Then I met the *Diana* here in New Orleans as she was about to get goin' back upriver to St. Louis. If I hadn't been able to get to my buckskins," I paused. "And my brother's knife an' tomahawk, I woulda found ya and hurt ya myself."

Billy leaned back, away from the cover of the bandstand, closed his eyes tight, and let the rain fall on his face. He stood up straight and shook his head, spraying water all around.

"You owe me." I grabbed the bottle, took another drink, and handed it back. "They tied me to a chair and was goin' to drown me in the river."

"How'd you get away?" he asked sheepishly.

"They carried me to the edge a' this cliff lookin' south to Natchez. I watched the *Diana* leave on down the river. I was part a' some ritual. After they tossed that fella Murrell shot into the water an' with all his men watchin', I grabbed Frenchy's knife from his belt and jumped. I hit the water an' the chair broke to pieces . . . Hell, I think he wanted me to get away."

Billy set the bottle on the rail and dug into his vest pocket. He pulled out a small leather bag and gave it to me. "This should do it, mate."

I poured eight ten-dollar gold pieces into the palm of my hand. I had never held that much money at one time. I handed five of the pieces back. He would not take it.

"Zeb, this ain't about money, it's about trust and I did leave you with that crazy bastard." He took a long swig and passed me the bottle. "I feel real bad, I do. Thing is, mate, I knew you'd make it out of there." Billy's eyes welled up a little. "They were throwing you in the bloody river?"

I nodded.

For a short while, there was silence between us. I was shocked at how much money I held in my hand.

"I can't remember, was she pretty?"

"The girl?"

He nodded.

"Wasn't no girl," I said.

He gave me a frown and asked nothing more.

Figuring he was about as contrite as I would ever see him, I put the bag of coins in my pocket. Besides, I was sure he won the money earlier that day in a card game and would probably lose it later that night.

The rain let up and we walked back through the arch.

The parlor thinned out as Sophie's girls took the hands of their rich clients and led them up the marble staircase. I was there, so to speak, with Sophie and did not want one of her whores, so I stood at the small bar with Billy and drank. Though, to save my life, I still did not trust him and swore to myself I never would.

"Who's your brother?" I asked.

He did not acknowledge my question and kept on drinking.

"Billy, who's your goddamn brother?"

From behind, someone cleared his throat.

"Gentlemen, may I join you?" Olgens Pierre asked.

Billy and I made room between us. I did not see Sophie or the Chinese woman anywhere in the parlor. Billy offered his bottle, which Olgens waved off. Instead, he ordered a bottle of Sophie's finest Scotch whisky from the barkeep, paying for it with two gold pieces. I touched the coins I held in my breast pocket and glanced to Billy. He smiled and nodded.

"Gentlemen, let me pour you a drink."

I had never tasted Scotch whisky before. Nor had I ever stood so close to a Negro. Olgens Pierre looked to be in his late thirties, though I could not tell for sure. He was a tall man, taller than Billy or me, tight in his demeanor and fit, like a fighter. His skin looked as if someone had painted on dark chocolate and his eyes were as black as Sophie's was. He smelled like clean smoke.

"Shall we toast?" he asked after pouring the drinks. He spoke with no accent except for a slight lilt at the end of his sentences. I had no idea where he might be from.

We joined Olgens in raising our glasses.

"To great friends and bitter enemies, may we always know the difference."

"Here, here, mates!"

I did not say anything and drank the Scotch. It tasted of oak and fire all the way down. I resisted coughing and gently laid the glass on the bar.

I wanted another drink.

"Zebadiah. May I call you Zebadiah?"

I nodded.

"It is now time we talk," Olgens said firmly but in a low voice, looking around for any eavesdroppers.

Again, I nodded.

"I have an interest, as you do, in, shall I say, the detainment or worse of two men who are, unfortunately for us, to be found in plain sight. They walk the streets of New Orleans with impunity." He paused to catch his breath. "Some say, with the hand of the law guiding them."

I cleared my throat. "May I call you Olgens?"

"Why, of course, sir."

"Well then, Olgens, two men I'm lookin' for, I'm goin' to kill 'em both. In plain sight or otherwise." It felt as if I slurred the words.

He gave a surprised look, then promptly recovered his composure. "Zebadiah, this is not St. Louis, sir. And while I appreciate our common enemy's ultimate fate, here in New Orleans, your indiscretions may get you hanged."

"Sir, did one of 'em shoot yer brother in the head?" I turned to face him square, standing inches from his face.

He lowered his eyes but held his ground. "My condolences for your brother's demise. I know how you must feel, for I too have lost loved ones to these men." He glanced back up and held my gaze. "While I regret your brother's death, ending up at the end of a rope will, how shall I say, exacerbate your problem, sir . . ."

I did not know the word *exacerbate,* but it did not sound good. I backed off.

Olgens poured another round. I gulped mine down. I winced as Billy hit me on the shoulder. "We keep drinking this, mate, an' we'll soon be wearing bloody kilts!" He bent forward laughing, slapping his knee. I had no idea what he meant. Olgens did not find it funny, either. Billy looked at both of us, drank his Scotch, and was quiet.

"Olgens, sir, since you know why I want 'em dead. What do they got on you?" I asked.

He set his glass on the bar and bowed his head. "Mr. Brody was my partner, of sorts.

Until last month . . ." One at a time, he slowly clenched both hands into fists. "He sold something that was not his to sell." He did not look up. "A person. Persons. A woman and two children, brothers, he sold them all back into slavery."

My head began to swim. The more he talked, the more I felt a darkness pull me backward, toward memories long forgotten. The words had not yet come out of his mouth before *an elk-hide strap tightens around my skinny neck. My brother, so young, cannot keep up and is dragged behind the horse like an animal. Forced to walk through the dark, windswept prairie, miles and miles until we are tied to a stake behind a teepee. Still with our mother and father's blood on our clothes.*

I could not say if it was the strong Scotch whisky that caused my vision or because of everything that had happened from the time of Jonathan's death. Somewhere deep inside of me, a dam broke open. My hands began to shake and I tried to speak but could not. I did my best to hide my feelings with another drink.

Olgens continued his story.

"I bought them through Brody, as I cannot own slaves myself. He kept them for a time, in a safe location, until they could be

215

spirited away to freedom in Haiti, my home." Olgens poured more Scotch into his glass, swirled it around and around, then drank it down in one shot. "Her name is Margo. Two sons she has. I found them being sold at New Exchange. A prominent family was sailing for France and could not take them. Brody was my proxy, though it was my money used to buy them. I waited a long time for a chance to free her."

Billy stood silent, with a strange, sullen, almost disgusted look on his face, as if he had heard the story before.

I still felt the thin strap choking me.

"They were safe for a time, here, a few days maybe. Sophie saw to it. I had arranged for their passage to my country, though I could not be seen escorting them to the ship. Baumgartner handled that. This was two weeks ago." He stopped and cleared his throat. "Two evenings before tonight, at the corner of St. Louis and Charles Streets, I saw her."

"What do you mean you saw her?" I asked, though I sensed the answer.

"Following behind a man, a man of wealth and prestige, whose plantation lies northwest of the city. No chains were needed to know she was now his. I followed them as well as I could without being seen, until they were spirited away by carriage."

"We aim to take 'em back, mate."

"Back to where?"

"I will take them to Haiti," Olgens announced. "I will row the boat across the Gulf myself, if need be."

I could not ask another question, except one. "What about Brody?"

"Mr. Brody will die, by your hands."

"Baumgartner's the man who killed my brother, not Brody," I said.

"Then they both will die, and your brother's death is avenged," Billy stated matter-of-factly.

I set my glass down and looked at him square. "An' what the hell does a Brit care about these certain circumstances?"

He shrugged and said, "I despise slavery."

The wind blew open the front door. The three of us turned to see two men enter and begin brushing off their rain-soaked coats. One was bearded and as he removed his top hat, long gray hair spilled down to the middle of his back. He wore earrings in both ears and his left eye was crooked. As the last of Sophie's girls took his coat, he grabbed her and buried his face in her bosom. She giggled and immediately led him upstairs.

The other gentleman stood tall and gazed

around the near empty parlor, twirling his top hat in his right hand. He stopped when he lit on us and held the hat still, then stuck a finger through a shot hole three inches above the brim, as if to fondle it. The candlelight glistened off the top of his bare head. He showed near perfect teeth as he smiled up at Sophie coming down her marble and oak staircase.

"Sophie le Roux, ya got more goddamn niggers in this here whorehouse then ya got whores!" Baumgartner bellowed, and glanced back at us.

I reached for Jonathan's knife.

It was not there.

CHAPTER 22

Baumgartner went straight for Olgens. He nodded to Billy as if he knew him and did not acknowledge me but for a snort. Dressed in formal clothes and with my beard and hair cut short, I looked nothing like I did on the river that night. Gripping the edge of the bar to steady myself, I took a deep breath. I was at once very sober.

"*Monsieur* Baumgartner, a pleasant surprise it is to see you here!" Sophie stepped in front of him and attempted to catch his arm.

He shook her off. "I will have no woman tonight," he exclaimed and threw his hat on the bar directly behind of me. "I'll be a drinkin' though, here with my favorite nigger. An' his friends?"

We looked eye to eye. I could not disguise my utter hatred for him. He turned away.

"Billy Frieze, ya squaggle, you, how the hell are ya, *mate*?" He smiled. "Ya still hidin' from yer brother, ya are?" Not waiting for an answer, he picked up the bottle of Scotch and leaned over to Olgens. They were about the same height. "Mr. Pierre, you 'bout the richest bastard here at this bar. Hell, in this whole goddamn whorehouse more likely!" He held the bottle to the candlelight. "Only nigger I know can afford this!" His eyes narrowed on Olgens. "Pour me a drink."

Sophie went behind the bar and found a clean glass.

Olgens slowly reached for the bottle, took it from Baumgartner's hand, and poured Scotch into the glass. "Sir, I believe there is enough left for you. That is, if you are so inclined to drink with a nigger and his friends." He held the glass in front of him. "After all, my money buys the very same things your money does."

Baumgartner sloshed the Scotch down and gasped, "Goddamn man, that's good!" He held out the empty glass. "One more fer old timey's sake, partner?" Olgens poured more. "Fact is," Baumgartner continued, "ya got more money up yer ass than I ever had in my life."

"I hardly think so. May I propose a toast?" Olgens asked, holding the bottle out to Billy and me.

I stood dumbfounded staring at the three of them. I could not imagine having a toast with the man who killed my brother. Yet, I allowed Olgens to fill my glass.

Sophie stayed behind the bar and was quiet.

"To business gone good," Olgens pronounced. "And business gone bad. 'Tis the same, only business."

Everyone drained his Scotch but me. I slowly poured mine over Baumgartner's muddy boots. His show of surprise came at the same instant he recognized the small scar on my left cheek. Our eyes locked.

"You ain't dead," he sighed.

"No, sir, I ain't dead."

"You come all this way to kill me?"

"Yes, sir, I did." My skin crawled and my heart was at my throat, but my hands were steady as rocks.

"Mighty determined are ya?"

"I am."

"Ya armed with somethin' other than yer fingers an' toes?" He snickered.

"Nope."

"Then how ya gonna kill me?"

"With my fingers an' toes."

"An' what if I pull a pistol from my coat an' put a ball through yer head like I did that fuck of a brother a yours?"

221

"You won't."

"Won't pull a pistol?" He raised an eyebrow and slid his right hand toward the opening of his coat.

I kicked him hard, with the point of my boot, cracking his left kneecap. He went down to the floor on his other knee but still held the knife he pulled. I swiftly moved around to his backside and stomped him square between his shoulders. Though the wind must have been knocked out of him, he stood up, gasping, swirled to face me, clutching the knife in a fist, blade down, and took a swipe. I jumped back, into the main parlor. He followed and we began to circle each other in front of the staircase.

"You have my knife."

"Yours? Ain't yours, took this here knife from a dead man on the Missouri some months back."

He limped toward me, sweeping the blade in front of him quick, back and forth, like a sickle. I hit the first step and climbed backward, up three to gain height. From behind, I heard shuffling but dared not look around.

Glancing past me, Baumgartner did not smile so much as grit his teeth. "Ah, the good Gentlemen of New Orleans. Come away from fuckin' yer whores to watch?"

I kicked him in the gut.

He tried sucking in a breath then doubled over in front of me. I kicked at his throat and missed, kicking only his chin. Somehow, he held onto the knife and blindly took a swipe. I jumped to the floor. Circling to his left, I punched hard, hitting him in the ear, two, maybe three times. He kneeled at the first step, breathing slow, taking the beating.

I looked up for the first time. It seemed the stained-glass window was lit by some outside light. The moon in the doorway glowed. Below, crowded on the landing, a gallery of folks watched us fight. Most all the men and their ladies were in various stages of undress. I could not understand what they all were saying though the jest seemed to be that some were making bets on the winner, who would be the last man alive. I heard Baumgartner's name several times, not knowing whether they were cheering him on, or wanting him dead. It did not matter to me what they said.

I glanced at my thigh. There was blood, but I did not feel the cut.

Billy and Olgens were still at the bar.

Sophie was gone.

Baumgartner took a wheezy breath and tried to stand straight but could not. "Gonna have ta do better if yer gonna kill this old dog." He turned to me, his face nearly the color of a beet. "So far, ya just pissed me off, ya fuck turd. I'm gonna run ya through like I shoulda let Rudy do ya!"

He flipped the knife in his palm and came at me, thrusting then slashing, with me dodging him as we circled.

He stopped and let his knife arm drop. "Hell, I just realized. You'd be dead now if I hadn'ta stopped him from cuttin' yer throat." He thought for a second. "I saved yer goddamn life ya piece a' shit and now ya want ta kill me?" He looked as if his feelings were truly hurt.

I stayed crouched in my fighting stance. "You killed my brother."

"Yer brother was already dying, son. I did him a favor a not sufferin' too much longer."

I thought for a second that his words might be genuine and eased slightly.

Baumgartner thrust.

With both hands, I grasped his wrist and pulled him swiftly into me, down, slamming to the floor, him on top. With a thwack, the knife stuck hard in the wood floorboard at my side, the sudden shock causing him to let go of the handle. I struggled to roll him over but could not. With my arms pinned by his long legs, he grasped my throat, his fingers choking me, pressing all his weight down, blood oozing from his right hand where the blade must have cut him. I felt for the knife with one hand while with the other, pulled back one finger at a time, snapping two. No matter, he did not let up.

"You . . ." He clinched his perfect teeth as if they would break, spittle dripping onto my face. With every word, he slammed my head against the floor. ". . . did not have ta come here!"

A shadow fell on us from behind.

Father says, "Prepare my son, the dark angel cometh."

I closed my eyes, waiting for fireflies to guide me to my brother.

As if it were a dream, the deer antler handle of my knife was laid gently in the palm of my left hand.

Baumgartner stiffened and released his grip. I opened my eyes to see him clutch his own throat, gurgling, staring down at me in shock, the knife blade stuck through his neck then pulled back quick. I closed my eyes again, for blood was draining onto my face.

I did not know how many seconds I lay there, under his heavy, bleeding body. When I came to, Olgens Pierre leaned down and whispered in my ear, "You owe me, sir." He

glanced up at the now silent crowd still on
the landing, and was gone.

CHAPTER 23

The words sounded hollow, spoken from somewhere above me, as if I was lying at the bottom of a grave.

"The bastard had it comin'."

It could have been Billy speaking low as he rolled the body off me. Or maybe it was two or three of the good New Orleans gentlemen whispering together as they stood on the first couple of steps of the staircase watching Baumgartner bleed to death. Hell, I may have said those words.

I sat up coughing and felt my neck. Though there was blood, it was not mine and nothing seemed to be broken. I still held my knife.

I lay back and stared past the stunned faces of Sophie's customers, to the stained-glass window. The moon no longer glowed. It was as if the whole room had dimmed.

"Zebadiah."

I did not answer.

"Zebadiah, we must go now," Sophie whispered. "The questions have begun and we must go."

The man with the crooked eye leaned over Baumgartner, placed a finger under his nose and waited for a breath. He looked right at me, then Billy and shook his head. "Your brother ain't gonna be too happy 'bout this. That you was here fer this." He shook his head again and I thought I caught a smile. "Didn't figure on anybody killin' this tough old bastard," he said, with more whim than regret.

Billy faced his acquaintance. "The only way my brother's gonna know I was here is if you tell him you saw me here, Eddy."

"What I saw was a goddamn Nigger hand a white feller a knife to kill another white feller." Eddy frowned and looked down at Baumgartner. "Somebody's gonna pay, the nigger or the white feller. Maybe both. Now, the nigger's gone, skeetered out the back like a chicken shit. But the white feller . . ."

I tried sitting and with Billy's help, stood on my own.

I turned to Eddy. "Killed him fair."

"Matter of opinion, mister."

Billy and I almost touched shoulders. I clutched my knife and he held his hands in his coat pockets. Eddy casually rubbed his right palm on the handle of his knife and began to laugh. "Mr., you all covered in blood like that, wore out from fightin'. Hell, nearly dyin's what I saw. You gonna take me?" He looked at Billy and scoffed. "You ain't shit, Billy, you fuckin' drunk."

A click, then another click, as if a pistol had been double-cocked. Billy held the smallest double-barreled gun I had ever seen pointed right at Eddy's head.

"Ain't very large, mate. But I suppose it will blow your bloody face clean off."

Eddy turned and looked up at the landing. The crowd of gentlemen was gone, discreetly escorted, I suppose, out some back passage then around to their carriages. The only one left was young Juliette. She held an old flintlock pistol pointed at him.

Sophie stood at the open front door. "Edward Jacks, it appears to be your move."

"Time will come, Billy Frieze. Time will come," Eddy said, facing us. He took one last look at Baumgartner, snatched his hat from Sophie, and walked out into the rain. She closed the door gently, locked it, and stood facing her marble staircase and parlor, now quiet, with a dead man lying on the floor in a pool of blood. She shook her head in disgust.

I reached down and gathered in my hand

what little hair Baumgartner had. I scalped him, cutting the back of his head and peeling the skin forward. With another cut above the forehead, I pulled his scalp off and tucked it into my belt. I did not care what anyone thought, I deserved my prize and I took it.

I did not sing him a death song.

"Who's your brother?" I asked as I scrubbed blood off my face.

Billy sat back on the bed, head lowered, with a bottle squeezed between his legs.

I kicked the mattress. "Who's your goddamned brother?"

He looked up. "Figured you might kill him, not scalp him."

"It's my way . . ." There was no mirror in Sophie's sleeping room. "Is the blood gone?"

He ignored me. "So every man you killed, you scalped?"

"Don't mean nothin' to them. Means everything to me." I laid the soaked cloth on the edge of the water bowl. "It's who I am."

Billy nodded. "It's who you are . . ."

"Yer brother, Billy?" I kicked the mattress again, harder. Whiskey sloshed out of the bottle onto Billy's britches. He did not seem to notice.

"He's my half-brother."

The door clicked behind me. I spun around and pointed my unloaded pistol at Sophie.

"You must come with me now," she said with panic in her voice.

"I'm still covered in the bastard's blood."

"No matter, *Monsieur* Brody is down the stairs with several men, including Jacks, to gather the dead man's body and to take him away. And, he's wanting you . . ." Not able to stand still, she paced back and forth in front of the door.

With dead calm, I stood staring out the window, to the black, rainy night. Time seemed to mean nothing. My deed was done. With Baumgartner dead, I saw no reason to stay in New Orleans. I pulled out the doctor's travel case and opened it up on the bed.

"Zebadiah, there is no time, if they find you, they will kill you." Sophie pleaded.

It mattered none to me what she said. In seconds, I stripped off the blood-soaked clothes and pulled on my buckskins. I slipped my moccasins on then placed my knife, Frenchy's knife, and my brother's tomahawk in my belt. I loaded the pistol, swearing never to be caught un-armed again.

"Mate, she's right, they will kill you." Billy stood in front of me.

I looked at him and took a long breath, then to Sophie I said, "Figure I'll be goin'." She had stopped pacing and stared at my belt, as if she saw something in the dull shine of the steel.

"You must leave that here." She gently pushed me aside, picked up the travel case, and slid it under the bed. "Where did you get that?" she asked calmly, pointing to Frenchy's knife. Her piercing black eyes showed more than the fear of the evening's events.

Juliette appeared at the door. With a frantic look she gave Sophie two or three signs with her hands and fingers then pointed to the dark hallway. I heard foot-steps on the stairs below and men's angry voices echoing up the back passage.

"We cannot go there," Sophie whispered. She shut and locked the door. The muffled voices were getting closer.

"I can meet 'em in the hallway," I exclaimed.

Sophie strode to the wall opposite the window and shoved her hip against it. A piece of the wood panel gave way to reveal a secret passage. Juliette ducked through the hole. With only her hand showing, she summoned me to follow. Sophie pushed me toward her. "My Juliette will take you to a safe place." The men were pounding at the door.

"You must go!"

I laid a hand on my pistol. Part of me thought I could stand and fight. The truth, I was wrung out and was not yet ready to die. I entered the low, narrow passage. As Juliette silently closed up the wall, I saw Sophie jump on the bed with Billy. Seconds later, there was a crash, then silence. Through the wood, I heard Sophie say, "*Monsieur* Brody, you broke my door."

I followed Juliette between the walls of the rooms to an enclosed staircase. In total darkness, we spiraled down three stories to the kitchen and out the back door. Staying in the shadows, we walked around the side of the house to Liberty Street. A carriage sat in front with the driver leaning against one of the porch pillars, out of the rain. With my arm around Juliette, we stepped into the muddy street. The man came off the porch blowing a whistle. Juliette grabbed my sleeve and tried to run. I stopped and pulled my pistol, took aim, and shot him.

We ran the rest of the way to the wharf

where a small boat lay moored. Two hooded men stood ready to shove off. I hesitated, watching Brody and Jacks burst out of Sophie's front door and go to their driver lying in the street. Another man slowly walked to the edge of the porch and stood there. He was not looking at the three men, he was looking toward the wharf at us.

It was Billy.

With help from one of the boatmen, I joined them and we were pushed away from land. Soon, the lamps of Sophie's house disappeared among the black trees of the swamp.

CHAPTER 24

I had never before seen a lizard as large as a keelboat. With a rope strung around the massive body, it hung upside down from a tree near the shack. The heavy, spiked tail drooped down well past its bound back feet. The snout took up most of its head with rows and rows of jagged, pointed teeth that gleamed brighter than the pale light of dawn.

I stood with my head cocked, staring at the monster. The old Negro man slouched beside me.

"Na this here gata, he be mean sum bitch. Took me year ta catch him." He held up his left arm, wrapped in some kind of long grass. "Took hisself a' 'lil bite 'fore I kilt him." He shuffled over and stuck a finger into a small slit on its head. "Ya know how ya kill a gata?" The old man placed the crumpled, bloody finger to the middle of his own forehead. "With a knife, right 'tween the eyes."

"Like killin' a bear, 'cept you go for its heart."

He turned sideways to face me. "Son, you kilt a bear?"

"No . . . but my brother has."

"Yer brother's a mighty man," he stated and walked slowly toward the shack, motioning me to follow. "Hungry?"

I had not eaten since Juliette served me supper the evening before. I was also bone tired for I had traveled all night through the swamp.

"Yes, sir, I am."

The man stopped. "Son, don't you never call me sir 'gain, hear?" Without glancing back, he walked onto the porch and into the shack.

I stood alone, surrounded by the skins of skunks, muskrats, and minks. The smell of stale blood and salt filled the air. *Gata* hides of all sizes lay piled up at the side of the porch, some with their head and teeth still attached and some with tails simply hacked off. Right at the edge of the clearing was a heaping pile of bones, most I did not recognize. Though I did not know who the old Negro was, I felt strangely akin to him and his ways.

"Come on in, son," he hollered from the shack.

I stepped onto the porch and felt it move a little. I was not used to a house built on stilts out over the water. I smelled biscuits and seemed to forget everything except for how hungry I was.

But for the fire burning in a small stone fireplace, the only light in the shack shone through a smoke hole in the thatched roof. A single beam shone down onto the lower body of another man, dressed in clean, pressed trousers. The rest of him was in shadow. I pulled my knife.

"You look most natural wearing those buckskins, Mr. Creed." Olgens Pierre leaned into the sunlight and smiled. "Quite the armament you wear around your waist."

I stumbled, catching myself in a fish net hung near the door. Olgens swiftly stood and managed to keep me from falling head first into the fire. After I settled into a low-slung chair, the old man handed me a bowl of what looked like a biscuit covered in white corn mush. "These here is grits," he said and moved to the shadows near the back of the shack.

Olgens sat back down and watched me eat. After a while, he asked, "How long have you known Sophie?"

My eyes adjusted to the sunlight that streaked through cracks in the walls. All around me, different kinds of plants hung from the ceiling. Three dead chickens were strung together and hung by the open window. Flies buzzed all around them. It smelled of smoke, blood, mold, and fish. Olgens sat across from me on the other side of the fireplace. He seemed not to be the same person he was the night before. Still seated in shadow, his eyes reflected the fire.

"You got outta there quick," I mumbled with a mouth full of grits.

"Had to, they would have killed me outright."

I nodded. "Suppose so."

"How long have you known Sophie?" he asked again.

"Why'd you help me?"

"I had no choice, he was killing you."

I looked away, glanced back to him, and then looked away again. It was a hard truth to swallow that a man had gotten the best of me, and by his two hands, I was on my way to dying.

"Two years," I answered.

"Have you shared her bed?"

I remembered her dance and song two nights before, her standing naked, with me in a trance, obliged to do only her bidding.

Flashes of wind, rain, flesh, sweat, and heat flooded my mind. There was no love in our acts, only passion and lust.

"Of course."

Olgens shook his head. I could not tell if he wore a smile or a frown.

The old man took my empty bowl and threw it into a pot of water sitting outside the door, stepped off the porch, and disappeared.

"What's it matter, her and I? She's been with so many men ya couldn't even count."

At this, Olgens did smile and nodded in agreement. "Indeed, maybe thousands."

"Let me ask you a question, why's a Negro like yourself tied in with a woman like her?"

He hesitated. Then, "She is my sister."

I slid back in my chair as he leaned forward into full sunlight. At first, I saw nothing. Then slowly, there came a resemblance, the same high cheekbones and short nose. Though her skin was light and his dark, they both had the same piercing, black eyes. I was reminded of a young girl who had eyes as black. She lived in St. Louis, in a whorehouse with her father.

"Why the secrecy, then?" I asked.

"It would not be good for business if folks knew, for her or for me."

I had one more question. "Why are you telling me this?"

"Because you are the one who will help us."

"Me?"

"Yes, Mr. Creed, you."

"How?"

"You will help Sophie keep her place of business out of Benjamin Brody's hands. And, you will help spirit away our brother's wife and children, back to Haiti with me."

"Why should I do these things?"

"As I said last night, after handing you your knife, you owe me, sir."

I sank deeper into the chair. I had gone to New Orleans to kill one man, two if Brody should get in my way. Though I was certainly grateful to be alive, I had not asked for any of this retribution.

"An' if I should walk on outta this shit swamp, an' leave this mess behind?"

Olgens shook his head. At the door, the old man began to laugh, a cackling sound, like a rooster deep in the forest. "Son, I get lost in this here swamp an' I live here most a' fifty year now," he said, continuing to laugh.

"Pawpaw is right; you will not get out alive." Olgens pointed toward the door, to the lizard, the *gata* hanging from the tree.

240

"Mr. Creed, there are many more where he came from." Looking outside, I could see its tail hanging almost to the ground.

Sunk I am, deep in the mud of this goddamn black water. No way out but through their good graces . . . I stood and stretched, my hands almost touching the ceiling of the shack. Olgens also stood.

"I'll do your bidding, seems I have no choice."

"Ah, Mr. Creed, there are many choices one may make. It's choosing the right and honorable path that brings us to triumph."

Somewhere inside of myself, I knew he spoke the truth. I felt it time to change the subject of our conversation.

"Why don't you have an accent, like your sister?"

Olgens smiled. "I learned a long time ago, sir, not to give away where I come from."

I thought for a second about my failed attempts at disguising who I really was. "Truth is," I offered, "a man always shows himself, sooner or later." Jumping into the pit to try to save Brigham came to mind. I absently touched the handle of Frenchy's knife.

"Ah, yes, but the prudent man will show himself by his own will, not by circumstance." He paused to catch my eye. "Are you a man of prudence, Mr. Creed?"

I was not sure what prudence meant. I merely nodded in agreement. Olgens also nodded, though with a look of disbelief that I knew anything of what he spoke. He leaned his head back and laughed out loud, cackling like the old man. After wiping tears from his eyes he said, "Zebadiah, a hungry, young panther you are, chasing the marsh birds that simply fly away. Prudent is the alligator that rests silent in the water all day, until the bird lands gently on its snout. Then . . ." He clapped his hands together, right at my nose. *"Snap!"*

I jumped. The old man and Olgens laughed together, slapping each other on their backs until they both stood facing me, out of breath.

"How did ya say you killed the *gata*?"

"Right 'tween the eyes!" They both shouted, making stabbing motions with their hands.

I nodded and smiled.

Through the afternoon and evening, I slept. Olgens and the old man seemed to come and go without much mind to me snoring in a hammock near the rear of the shack. Between fitful sleep and lying awake in the dark, I thought I heard my brother, right

242

outside, cutting, scraping, and stretching hundreds of beaver hides. Early the next morning, as dawn was breaking, I woke to the familiar putrid smell of a tub of fat boiling into tallow. It must have been cut from the alligator, for when I glanced outside, the monster no longer hung from the tree.

The grits were better than the morning before. Maybe the food and the smells were growing on me, as were Olgens Pierre and his grandfather. After fishing all afternoon along the banks of the bayou, they took me out at twilight, hunting for *gatas.* We did not see a one.

That evening, we fried up the catfish and croakers we had caught and ate them along with greens and chopped cattail roots. After the fine supper, Olgens offered up a pipe and a bottle. As we sat around the fire, he told me a story.

"We came as boys to this swamp, my brother and I, from Haiti around 1800. Not far from here is where we grew up, south toward the gulf 'tween Terre Bonne and Barataria, in a village hidden away from the rest of the world." He paused to take a puff off his pipe. "Born free we were, and have stayed free. Pa and Pawpaw as well."

"Barataria?"

"Lafitte's kingdom. Today it is in ruins,

but in the day was quite prosperous, for valuable goods and slaves . . . stolen and resold."

"Who is Lafitte?"

Olgens stared at me in disbelief. "You have not heard of the famous buccaneer Jean Lafitte?"

I thought for a second then said, "Nope, can't say as I have. Who is he?"

"The last of the great captains he was. His own man, free from any government in the world, except for the one he built with his own hands and blood, I'm afraid. Made up of seafaring swaggards the likes that Grand Terre or the whole of Louisiana will never see again." He took a drink. "My brother and I ran goods for his operation, to Haiti and back we would go, selling all kinds. Is how we made our fortune and bought the property we," he stopped. "I own . . ."

"What's his name?"

"His name was Jean, Jean Pierre."

"I'm sorry," I whispered and bowed my head. "The death of my own brother is still fresh."

"It would seem, sir, that time heals, but it does not. And your brother?"

I looked up, not understanding the question.

"His name, what was his name?"

"Oh. Jonathan, Jonathan Creed."

"Jonathan Creed," he said slowly. "Strong name."

I nodded in agreement.

Olgens continued. "We were the only two freed men Lafitte trusted. Most Negroes he knew only as slaves that he and his men stole off Spanish ships and sold upriver, some as far away as Natchez and Memphis.

"Jean Pierre took a wife, paid good money for her as she was bound for one of the northern plantations. He freed her and built a house on the east end of Grand Isle, across the inlet from Grand Terre, where Lafitte's fortress lay." He paused. "They had two boys and lived happy, until . . ."

Though I listened, I was lost as to why he was telling me a story about a man I would never know.

". . . Until Lafitte up and disappeared."

Olgens stood and went to the door to peer into the darkness. It had begun to rain for the first time since I had been at the shack. There was no sound but for a muffled moan from the trees. The air became so moist I could taste the black water of the swamp by licking my lips.

"With Lafitte gone, my brother and his family were left in the hands of fate and a murdering horde of brigands." He continued to stare into the black. "By the time I arrived back from my business in Haiti, Grand Terre had burned and so had Jean's home on Grand Isle. I found his body hung from a tree. I did not find Margo or their sons. I could not stay in Barataria or even Terre Bonne else the murderers might come for me. Later, in New Orleans, with Sophie, word came that they had been sold into slavery. Where and to whom, we did not know."

He stopped and took a breath, as if he was breathing in the whole of the swamp he knew so well. "For my own life, I retreated back to Haiti. There, I continued to build my business. I am a rich and powerful man, Mr. Creed." He pinched the chocolate skin of his right cheek. "Whoever I am in Haiti, here in America, I am only a nigger."

Again, I was confused as to why he was telling me this. "When did this happen?"

"The fall of twenty-four."

"Eleven years ago," I said under my breath.

"Yes, eleven years I have searched for Margo and her sons, with Sophie, then later, with Billy's help, of course."

"Billy, of course," I grumbled.

"He found them. Last year it was. In secret, he sent for me. It took until a few

246

months ago to make the necessary arrangements for their freedom." With his head hung low, he turned and one at a time, squeezed his hands into fists. He looked up at me with the blackest eyes I had ever seen and said, "You know the rest, sir."

The old man appeared at the door and nodded to Olgens. With a sudden sense of urgency, they both went to the rear of the shack. From under a tarp, they pulled two pistols and a shooting bag. The old man smiled a toothless smile and said, "Buck up, son, c'pany's comin'!"

It was then I heard the bell.

The rain must have dampened its first rings for me not to hear it, or I was simply distracted by Olgens's talk. No matter, if there were to be a fight, I was ready.

We left the fire burning inside and hid in the trees with two strides between us, in a half-circle around the shack. The intruders would be trapped in the open between the shore and the porch.

Across the water and through the rain, a ghostly light grew into a single oil lamp swaying gently at the bow of a shallow boat. I could make out three people, one standing with a long pole in his hand and the other two kneeling, ready to jump ashore. I aimed my pistol at the first one off the boat.

There came a sharp whistle, then, "Olgens, it's me, your *chere soeur,* come to take our friend to the opera, to at long last meet Benjamin Brody."

I held my aim on Sophie for a few long seconds, then lowered my pistol and stepped out of the trees, into the open rain.

Chapter 25

I stood next to the bed, naked, abruptly awakened, with my loaded pistol pointed at the Chinese woman. She sat straight, in a chair beside Sophie, at the low table, with the water pipe in front of them. They were not in the room when I lay down to sleep earlier in the day.

Except for the patched hole in the door, the room looked the same as it had when I arrived from Natchez four nights before. The travel case was still under the bed and untouched. The cracked window shut out most of the blustery afternoon wind and rain. Winter was coming to New Orleans, for a chill was in the air.

Sophie turned to the Chinese and raised her eyebrows, then turned back to me. "*Ma cherie,* a bit bigger you were the last I saw you with your trousers off." She had transformed from my courageous rescuer back to her frivolous self.

The Chinese acted embarrassed by placing a hand over her mouth. She did not hide her smile very well at all. Her name was Woo. I did not know her last name or if she even had one.

"Do you understand English?" I asked as I lay the pistol on the table and began pulling my britches on.

"Oui," she said with a flawless French accent.

Sophie reached over and stroked Woo's straight black hair, then gently caressed her small breasts, one after the other. With the top of her loose dress fallen open, Woo leaned slightly into the tips of Sophie's thin fingers and closed her eyes.

"This evening, upon returning from the opera, you are welcome to share her with me. If you dare . . ." Her glance to me was one of endearment.

I could not help but smile at the offer.

With a wave and a bow, Sophie shooed the young Chinese woman out of the room.

"Where does she come from?"

"Ah, from far, far away, across the western ocean." Sophie started giggling, like one of her young girls. "If she is Chinese then she be from where?"

"I honestly don't know."

She clapped her hands with glee. "From

China, of course! She came with Olgens, back from his long travels. Was given to him by the Emperor himself, or so he tells the tale."

"She is his slave?"

"Oh, no, Zebadiah, she is his concubine."

I still did not understand.

Her glance back to me was not one of sympathy for being ignorant of such things, but one of shock. "His mistress. How can you not know this?"

"And why do you offer her to me then?"

"When he is there, in Haiti, with his wife and children, she must survive here with me." She leaned over and caressed my cheek. "And after this evening, with what you must do, you will need her . . . as well as I."

"But Olgens is here."

"No *ma cherie,* he is far away, in the swamp, where we left him last night, with Pawpaw."

That I did understand. "You would do that to your brother?"

At this she laughed, hard, holding her stomach. "Oh, Zebadiah, I will not be fucking her, you will be."

Sophie sat in silence, watching me with a look of bemusement as I pulled my smock on.

"The opera?" I asked.

"I have made arrangements for you to be my escort this evening. It is the premier of *Le Postillon de Lonjumeau* at our fabulous *Théâtre d'Orléans*. My lovely Juliette will come to groom and dress you. You must look your best, Zebadiah, for tonight you meet *Monsieur* Benjamin Brody."

Before I could say a word, she raised a finger to her lips and said, "You will know what you must do."

A knock came at the door. Juliette entered carrying a set of men's clothes, very much like the ones she brought to me two nights earlier, and laid them out on the bed. She left the room and returned with a beaver top hat the likes I had never seen. It was elegant and silky black, with a dark brown deerskin band and feather plume the color of deep purple, the same color of the curtains that hung down at the landing of Sophie's marble staircase.

"Try not to bloody these, *Monsieur* Creed, I am almost out of men's clothes your size." Sophie stood and strode to the door. "Our carriage departs at six, don't be late!" With that, she walked out, leaving the door wide open.

From a small handbag, Juliette pulled scissors and a comb. As I sat, she trimmed my hair, not too short, but more in style with the fashions of New Orleans. She then produced a straight razor and soap and proceeded to shave my face, leaving the beginning of sideburns. She wiped my cheeks and neck clean, then handed me a small mirror and stepped back.

"You ah a very han'some man . . ." Juliette stuttered. They were the first words I heard her speak. She bowed her head as if she was embarrassed.

I touched her chin with my finger and gently lifted her head up. "Thank you, my dear." I knew she was deaf and did not want to make it seem such a disadvantage.

"You remind me of my sister Cattie, the last time I saw her. She's also sweet and lovely," I said, smiling. Juliette shook her head as if she did not understand my statement, yet her face was beaming.

I looked at my own face in the mirror and almost turned away. Her shave and trim were magnificent for I had never seen myself look so well-to-do. Yet, the man who gazed back at me, with his steel-gray eyes and small scar on his left cheek, was a man I hardly recognized. I felt a deep, tired sadness I did not remember having the last I stared into my own eyes.

I set the mirror on the table, stood, and

pulled my smock back off. Juliette handed a starched, white shirt to me and with her assistance, I was dressed for the opera.

The ride was a short one, through dark, narrow streets of gravel and mud. The rain had slowed to a drizzle, leaving a whispered patter on the roof of the carriage. Sheltered as we were, I still felt the cold and wet on my face. I shivered and pulled the coat closer around me.

I was about to meet Benjamin Brody, the one who set in motion the reason my brother was dead, a man who seemed to be wanted dead by at least two of his enemies. I was not one. My taste for vengeance had been quelled by the deaths of the two men I met on the Missouri months earlier. Yet again, I found myself in a compromising situation with my own will and pride, beholden to a man whom I owed for killing his pet wolverine. Another man I owed who saved my life by helping me kill Baumgartner.

If I go my own way, I could be looking over my shoulder for the rest of my life. Though I did not know the man, Brody might likely not rest until he himself avenged his friend's death, exactly as I had done with the death of my brother.

Wearing only a light shawl to cover her bare shoulders, Sophie snuggled under my arm to keep warm, her eyes closed, rocking gently against me to the sway of the carriage. She seemed to be asleep, but I knew she was not.

We turned a corner and the opera house lit up before us. Sunk deep in the shadows of a dozen two-storied arches, stained-glass windows cast gleaming, colored light onto the boardwalk and carriages lined up in front. Four gold-crowned pillars, two on each side and two stories high, guarded the arching main entrance. I sat in quiet awe as we waited our turn to arrive, the folks before us each dressed in such proper fashion and promoting the most elegant of manners. I glanced to Sophie. She smiled and held a gloved finger to my lips.

The front attendant opened our carriage door, saw who we were, and motioned to our driver to pull on ahead. I was halfway out to speak with him when Sophie snatched the back of my coat. We were guided around to the side entrance. There was no one to offer assistance. With my heart racing, I stepped down, turned, and held my hand out. Madame Sophie le Roux looked ravishing as she stepped from the carriage, her face flush and beaming. Her red French silk and lace dress swayed to and fro as I escorted her through the foyer and into the crowded lobby. Most of the men she nodded to with a smile as they tipped their hats, but no woman would acknowledge her. With not a word spoken to anyone, we entered the theatre and took our seats.

The lamps were lowered and the orchestra began. Though I had never heard music so sweet yet at the same time dramatic, I paid little attention to it. All I could see were the backs of heads in front of me.

Which one was Brody?

Sophie nudged me to look up and to our right. In a small balcony, one story above us sat a young woman. With black hair tied back, her silver dress glowed from the soft light of a single lamp. She peered at the darkened stage through a set of eyeglasses she held up with a stick. Seated beside her must have been Mr. Benjamin Brody for I recognized the man named Jacks sitting directly behind him. The seat next to Brody's was empty. As I continued to gaze up at them, the stage brightened and the singing began. I paid no heed. Instead, I watched Jacks scan the audience. Our eyes met. He leaned into Brody, whispered to him and they both looked down to us. I nudged Sophie. She looked up, gave a slight wave, and smiled. The woman must have seen this for she turned to Brody. He pointed to the stage, as if telling her to watch the opera.

"She is lovely, don't you think, *Monsieur* Creed?" Sophie waved again.

Behind Jacks, in the shadows of the small balcony, the curtains parted. The silhouette of a man entered and casually sat next to Brody. He leaned into the soft light, caught my eye, and raised a bottle to me.

"Billy Frieze . . ." The words came as I started for the aisle. Sophie took hold of my jacket and pulled me back to my seat.

"You can do nothing now. Wait for the intermission and we will meet them in the lobby." She turned back to the stage and then leaned toward my ear. "Your first opera *ma cherie,* sit back and enjoy . . ."

I sat for what seemed hours, seething, sweating, gripping the handle of my knife so hard my fingers felt as if they might break. I despised the singing, for it was in French. The music ebbed and flowed, rising to such a pitch of disharmony I cringed. During the silences between scenes and applause, all I could hear was my own heavy breathing. I looked to Sophie, sitting there, enraptured by the drama and spectacle. I wanted to blame her for what I was about to do, but could not.

At last, the lamps were lit bright. We filed out of the theatre and into the lobby. Sophie touched my hand and led us through the crowd toward the stairs that led up to the balconies. I gently pushed her aside and stood square near the bottom step.

Throngs of people passed by. Some folks gave a questioning look while others, deep in conversation, ignored me. Jacks came first, clearing the way for Brody. Billy Frieze followed.

"And you know this woman from where?" Brody's wife inquired as she followed her husband down the stairs. She spoke with a very American accent.

Brody did not answer. He slowly took the last step to the carpeted floor of the lobby and stood directly in front of me by several feet. Jacks moved to my right, close to the side entrance from where we came in. Billy stayed on the stairs, a few feet above us all.

Standing at Brody's side, his wife glanced at Sophie, then to me and back to him. "Dear husband, shall there be introductions, then? We shant stand here all intermission without a word between us." She did not seem at all nervous.

Again, Brody ignored her.

"Mr. Creed, I see you have survived your

journey through our paradise."

I was not sure what he meant. "If you speak of the shit swamp I've spent the last two days and nights in, well, sir, it ain't no paradise."

He smiled. "I was being facetious, sir. I too find it to be, as you say so eloquently, a 'shit' swamp." He glanced at Jacks. "Is why I rarely go there, anymore. Some years ago, I resided south, near where the fresh water opens to the salt of the gulf. There, I find the cool breezes of the open sea refreshing, ay, Mr. Jacks?"

"Yes, sir." Jacks answered without taking his crooked left eye off me.

"Brother Billy, did you enjoy the cool ocean breezes of our beloved Barataria?"

Billy did not answer.

I stared only at Brody but with enough sight to know where Jacks was. As he slowly moved out of my side vision, I stepped backward, pushing the gathering crowd into the center of the lobby.

Brody's wife stomped her tiny foot. "Husband, I demand introductions!"

I broke my stare to glance at her. A beautiful woman she was, maybe twenty-five years in age. Her black hair and high cheekbones reminded me of a younger Sophie. Both women seemed to be doing their best to ignore the other.

"Forgive me, my dear, for I have been so rude. Standing to our right is the illustrious Miss Sophie le Roux, proprietor of the finest bordello in all of New Orleans!" He waved his hand, as if brushing off the folks standing behind me. "Why, most of these good men here have visited at least once, with some of them being very regular patrons . . ."

A collective gasp rose up from the husbands and their virtuous wives. Sophie kept a stone face.

Brody burst out laughing. "Joking, mates, just joking."

Only the men laughed, nervously.

He continued. "Miss le Roux, may I introduce my new wife, the Mrs. Katharine Brody. Formerly, Miss Van Dorman of New York City, come here to share in my ever-developing entrepreneurships and, shall I say, certain risks that have paid off handsomely." He pulled a cigar from his breast pocket, snipped it, and snapped his fingers. "Ah, but some say I boast too much of my achievements."

Billy silently moved to a lamp and lit a punk. As his cigar lighted up, Brody gave a slight nod to Jacks.

I could feel from behind some of the

crowd dissipating, perhaps because the second half of the opera would soon begin.

Jacks stood still near the door.

"And who is the gentleman?" Mrs. Brody asked, raising an eyebrow. "He seems to not be from around here."

"Dear, word has it that he is a true mountain man, come from the Rockies all the way down the Missouri and Mississippi rivers to join us here this evening."

"And what is your name?"

"Creed, ma'am, Zebadiah Creed." I removed my hat and bowed.

She grinned and clapped her gloved hands together. "Oh, my, what a strong name! Don't you think so, Husband?" Not waiting for an answer, she asked, "What brings you to New Orleans, Mr. Creed?"

"Yes, Mr. Creed, what brings you so far away from your mountains?" Brody took a draw from his cigar, looked me up and down, blowing smoke my way. "Shouldn't you be wearing some sort of deerskin hides?"

No one laughed at this but Jacks.

"What do you say, Billy? You seem to have traveled with Mr. Creed for some time now, does he fit better in deerskin hides or these dandy clothes he wears tonight?"

Billy stood silent.

Brody swiftly turned to him. "I asked you a question, brother."

I gritted my teeth and started to reach for the knife I wore under my coat, then thought better of it.

"Buckskin, the traditional dress is called buckskin," Billy answered.

One of the opera attendants stepped up to my right, rang a small bell, and announced, *"Messieurs, mesdames, l'opéra est sur le point de recommencer . . ."*

Before he finished his statement, Jacks was in front of him with his coat open showing a small pistol and knife at his belt. *"Monsieur,* the opera will start again when Mr. Brody and his party are back at their seats an' comfortable."

"Now, now, Edward, no need for harshness." Brody frowned as he acknowledged the man. "Sir, I beg you and the rest of the fine singers and players for five minutes of your patience to conclude our awkward business here."

Jacks did not move. The gentleman glanced to Sophie and me, then to Brody and back to Jacks. With a look of frustration and fear, he slowly backed away.

"Where are we now?" Brody took a step toward me. "Ah, yes, the real reason Mr. Creed is standing here this evening wearing these fine clothes, rather than his . . ." He glanced up to Billy. "Buckskins?"

"I like the singin' . . . and the playin'," I stated, frowning.

"I say, sir, that you are a liar."

I stood calm and offered no response.

"I say that you have come here to New Orleans to assassinate me."

The air in the lobby shifted, as if someone had hastily opened a door and immediately shut it again; even the smoke of Brody's cigar waivered. Everyone was quiet, waiting for my answer. His wife stared at me with not a look of fear, but with a gleam in her eye, as if she anticipated my next words. I stepped forward. Jacks moved toward me with his coat still open. Brody waved him off and took another step. We were within an arm's reach of each other.

Again, I offered no response, except to open my coat. Brody looked down to the plain wood handle of Frenchy's knife I wore at my waist.

Brody sneered. "Sophie, you bring him to me with idle threats?"

She offered no response.

"If I would'a followed suit with the demand of a certain whorehouse owner in St. Louis, you'd be dead now." I gritted my teeth and glared at Billy. "Your brother didn't tell 'bout the goddamn wolverine?"

Brody leaned toward Billy and said, "St. Louis is a little far south for wolverines, don't you think, Mr. Creed?"

"Thought so when I killed it with my knife blade, right through it's heart."

"Did you kill it with the knife at your belt?"

"Oh, no, sir, this knife Frenchy gave me, to kill you with."

Brody's face turned a shade red as he gave the briefest glance to Sophie.

"Do you recognize it?" I asked. "The knife, Mr. Brody? Frenchy claimed you once held it in your hand."

Brody's wife must have caught his glance to Sophie. She stomped her foot again. "Husband, I demand to know what you two are speaking of."

With some exasperation, he said, "Please, dear, bear with me."

"Ma'am, I've been told that your husband used this here knife, years ago, to cut a man . . ." I hesitated. "But could not kill him."

Brody's lips tightened into a grimace. His right hand clenched to a fist several times, as if he still held the knife.

Sophie began to choke, then cough, recovering after a few seconds.

"Mr. Creed . . ." Brody said slowly, as if he were gathering his thoughts. "Mr. Creed, you come to my city, kill my friend, leave my driver for dead in the street, and now you insult me with this accusation of cowardice?"

"Baumgartner killed my brother, he deserved to die." I turned slightly and glanced at Jacks. "Your driver got in the way."

The crowd behind me seemed to press in closer, to hear every word.

"Your brother can tell you more of Frenchy," I nodded. "They seem to know each other well enough. Fact is, your brother Billy here could speak for hours 'bout the business of Frenchy in St. Louie . . . an' beyond."

"Well, sir, I will keep that thought in mind."

I slid closer to Brody. "As I said, if I wanted to kill ya here, you'd be dead."

Jacks stepped closer to me with a hand on the handle of his pistol.

"*Monsieur* Brody?" Sophie spoke for the first time. "Benjamin, my dear, we both know Frenchy, and who is concealed behind the name. Do not be so coy, leading these good folks on." She faced Mrs. Brody. "Young woman, this situation, it is like an old wound that has not healed properly.

Perhaps *Monsieur* Creed has come here to help in its healing . . ."

I did not know of what she was speaking.

Jacks was within an arm's reach of me. I stood square, facing Brody.

The attendant from the opera stepped back into sight, rang his bell, and announced that the second half was to begin, with or without us taking our seats.

No one moved.

"Husband, I am curious about this man Frenchy . . ."

With the knife's handle, I struck Brody, shattering his nose. His wife stood frozen as blood splattered onto her face, hair, and dress.

I spun Brody around, holding the blade at his throat. Jacks could do nothing, else I would slice his boss's throat open.

"In order to regain your honor and respect," I whispered into Brody's ear, "I'm guessin' you'll be sendin' your second 'round to Sophie's sometime in the morning, challengin' me to a duel. In which case I'll accept, choosin' long knives as my weapon of choice. Knives similar to this one ya cut Frenchy with eleven or so years ago." I took a deep breath and stated out loud for all to hear. "You, sir, are a coward and liar."

I heard a double click from behind me.

Billy held his tiny double-barreled pistol on Jacks.

"Billy Frieze," Jacks spoke low. "You have chosen yer side fer the last time."

A couple of swift kicks and I hobbled Brody at the back of both knees, laying him out on the carpet. I sat down cross-legged with his head nearly in my lap. Dazed and with his light gray suit coat drenched in blood, his handsome face was already turning red and blue from his broken nose. I grabbed a hold of his chin and pulled it back toward me. Squeezing my fingers into his cheeks, he slowly raised his swelling eyes. "Look at me, you piece a shit," I whispered. "I want my goddamn furs back!"

With the tip of the knife, I cut his left cheek, deep and by an inch.

I stood as Mrs. Brody knelt down and franticly cradled her husband's head in her lap, crying for anyone to help. The crowd in the lobby had grown with the ruckus, yet no one lent a hand.

Billy followed us, close behind, his tiny gun still trained on Jacks. Sophie took hold of my arm and casually walked me out the front entrance.

Not a drop of blood was on my clothes.

CHAPTER 26

Sophie placed the flame of the candle to liquid. With a flash, the top of the glass turned green for an instant then a deep blue with a hint of flickering yellow. She blew out the flame and lifted the glass to her lips.

"Sugar to sweeten, fire to release the spirits!" she proclaimed and drained every drop.

We were in her entertaining room, she at the round mahogany table and me at the double bay windows. It seemed a thousand candles lit up the crystal chandelier. Directly above us, on the third floor was the room where I stayed. Earlier, she showed me a hidden passage between the two. The Madame and her house indeed had many secrets.

I turned to face the window and stared into the black swamp, as I had done the first night. This time, I knew what lay beyond the small wharf.

"I saw Baumgartner from the window above, the morning you and I rose together."

"There are many who travel our busy thoroughfare throughout the day and night. Are you so sure you are not mistaken?"

"Not on the street but at the boat landing across from this house."

She was silent for a moment then asked, "And what did you witness *Monsieur* Baumgartner doing, Zebadiah?"

I turned back to the room. She had let her hair down and lifted a flame-filled glass. Her eyes shined black diamonds.

I faced the window again. In the reflection of the glass, I could see her standing right behind me holding out the flaming demon in her hand.

"Quick, before the fire must be blown out," she whispered.

I tried to stay still, not to turn. Yet, as if she willed it, I spun around and reached for the drink, blew out the flame, and gulped it down. The instant the burning liquid touched the tip of my tongue, I knew she had snared me. It tasted of the sky, as if pure white clouds had been distilled, then mixed with the blackest of earth, down deep, in the pits of hell.

"The fire is quenched?"

I barely shook my head. "Only more

enraged . . ." The glass slipped from my fingers and fell onto the carpet without a sound. I felt that I might stumble if I took a step so I stood frozen, with my back to the window. The chandelier brightened behind Sophie. She became a shadow in a blood-red dress with a face as white as the clouds I had drunk. Her black eyes bore into mine as if she sought the true essence of my soul. I lifted my hands and with the tips of two fingers, caressed the scars left on my chest years before by the sun dance. I was no longer afraid of what she might find.

"You are the witch."

Her cackling laugh sent chills up my spine. She instantly became the old crone I accused her of being.

"Ah *ma cherie,* Frenchy has told you too much, and . . . not nearly enough."

She reached out, gently took both my hands, and pulled herself into me, pressing her body against mine, holding my fingers captive by her large, firm breasts. I closed my eyes for an instant and when I opened them, she was a young, voluptuous girl about Anna's age.

"I was his one true love."

"But not your only love," I mumbled, my tongue thick and numb. Though my vision shifted between the real and the unreal, somehow my mind was clear.

She let go of me and floated back to the table, picked up the gold bottle, and filled another glass. Not bothering to light the fire, she drank it down.

"There is still a life, between us." Her face changed before my eyes, from innocence to sorrow. She wavered, then slumped into one of the chairs and sat in silence, staring at the empty glass in front of her. After a few seconds, she turned her gaze back to me. "What is her name?"

"Sapphire."

"Named her after one of his treasured gems, *Monsieur* Lafitte did."

"Who?"

Sophie shook her head. "Ah, I am sorry, I meant Frenchy."

I had never seen a woman shift so deftly from that of a seductress, to a virgin, on to a haggard, old woman.

She let out a sharp hiss. A whiff of green mist slipped out of her mouth. "He stole my *bébé*, Jean did . . ." She stopped. "Frenchy. Frenchy took my *petit bébé* from me before I knew her name."

"And Brody?"

"A fucking coward, as you say." She spat out the words. "He cut Frenchy, but could not take his heart away."

271

"You loved him."

Sophie looked confused, then sat up straight in the chair. "*Monsieur* Creed, I loved them both."

The room began to swim around me. Frenchy's voice played in my ear, whispering, *Witch . . . a spell she spins and see what she gives to me.*

I reached for the edge of the table to steady my shaking hands and sat down. Sophie stared at me, her eyes blacker than two shadows. She became that little girl in St. Louis. *You will know my mère in New Orleans.*

I turned away and soon the spinning stopped. In a strong, clear voice, I heard . . . *I was the king of Louisiana, Barataria, and all the warm waters of the Caribbean. I come here, I build this from nothing in St. Louie, Frenchy's Emporium.*

The effects of the drink were gone.

"While in the swamp," I said, "a story was told to me by your brother. A man named Lafitte was mentioned . . . a very powerful man who disappeared eleven years ago?"

Sophie stayed still in her chair and cried.

"Your daughter, and Frenchy's, she's about eleven now, ain't she?"

Silence. She did not move but to wipe tears from her eyes.

I remembered something Frenchy said to Rudy seconds before he let the rope of the guillotine slip away. I quoted aloud. ". . . An' yet you run, as the tide runs 'long south *Terre Bonne,* in an' out, out an' in. Because the saw grass hides you, I can't keep up with my old friend. One day, the grass will cut my feet, trip me, drag me down. The hidden tide rushes in to drown me, even here, way upriver in St. Louie."

I stared at Sophie. "Did you know Rudy Dupree?"

She glanced over to me, surprised, her tears drying up. "I know a few men named Rudy." Her face turned a shade closer to the color of her red dress. "Why do you ask?"

"He was the man sent by Brody, with Baumgartner and another fella named Jeffery, to steal furs along the Missouri. I told you about 'em, remember? He lost his head, in St. Louis."

Again, she was silent. Only by a slight twitch in her left cheek did I sense a reaction.

"I thought you knew," I said.

She gathered her composure and in an instant became again the seductress. Pushing her chair away, she stood and reached for the ceiling as she did the first evening

273

we spent together, swaying her hips and humming a subtle tune under her breath. Her stark black eyes returned to stare at me. "The Chinese will be along any time now. We should drink more and prepare for her. She is quite the treat." Sophie shut her eyes and began feeling herself through her dress.

Several hard knocks came at the door.

"My dear sister, I know Mr. Creed is there with you. I must speak with him now for I have a delivery to make."

Sophie stopped dancing and slowly opened the door for Olgens. Without acknowledging her, he came straight to me. "Sir, I don't know how this has happened, but you have been summoned to appear tomorrow, at dawn, to a duel at the Oaks. Mr. Benjamin Brody will be waiting." He paused to catch his breath and to hand me a small business card. "Since he is the challenger, you will choose the weapons. And . . . You will need a second."

I stood reading the card, then without hesitation, looked up to Olgens. "Sir, I would be honored if you would be my second."

"There has never been a Negro that I've heard to have this role. However . . ." He stood straight and tall. "I am a free man to follow my own will. I, sir, accept your offer. I will now send a dispatch to Mr. Brody telling him that you will meet him at dawn. What weapons do you choose?"

Sophie had sat down and poured herself another drink. I supposed our evening together was about to be drawn to a close.

"Long knives, of course. The particular ones will be mine and my brother's, they are almost identical." I looked at the both of them. "Unless, Brody would choose Frenchy's knife?"

There were glances back and forth between the brother and his sister.

A shuffle of feet came from the hallway. The Chinese woman stood in shadow, a step outside the door. Olgens turned and waved her into the room.

"My friend, may I offer to you my consort. She was given to me by the Emperor himself. God forbid, if this be your last night on Earth, she will certainly make it worthwhile."

So tempted I was. Yet, deep inside I knew I would be overwhelmed with shame and guilt.

"Thanks for the offer. However, I am not in the habit of lyin' with slaves . . . 'Sides, I have knives to sharpen." I turned to Sophie. "Would you show me again the secret passage to the room upstairs?"

Sophie sat asleep in her chair. Olgens stared down at his shoes. He raised his head and without a look into my eyes said, "Sir, I will escort you upstairs to your room so you may prepare for the morrow."

The Chinese woman stood caressing Sophie's gray, black hair. With a bow, Olgens allowed me first out through the door.

CHAPTER 27

The early morning was colorless. Gray Spanish moss hung from the trees, reminding me of sad, old faces peering through the fog. Our driver guided the carriage slowly up the muddy road to a large patch of grass under ancient oaks, the favored dueling ground of most New Orleans gentlemen. As we were the first to arrive, I chose the spot where we would fight. My party was small, with only Sophie, Juliette, and of course Olgens, my second. Olgens set up a stand and case that contained two equal knives, one was my brother's and the other was mine. If Brody chose to, he could fight with Frenchy's knife, but I doubted he would.

My head pounded from the absinth drunk the night before. Yet, as the fog began to clear, I stood ready.

Minutes later two carriages pulled to a stop behind ours. From the first stepped Brody and his wife. From the other stepped

Jacks and a man I did not know. I assumed he was a physician. Jacks was dressed as he was the night before, still in his long coat. Brody was prepared to fight wearing a loose smock, leather trousers, and light brown knee boots. He wore a bandage over his nose. They did not seem so surprised to see me wearing my buckskin smock, britches, and moccasins. On my belt were six scalps held in a ring. The thinnest of them was Baumgartner's.

"Sir, you are certainly the mountain man this morning. Or shall I call you an American savage?" With Brody's nose broken, he sounded shallow and distant.

"You can call me anything you like," I squared up. "How's yer nose?"

"You caught me last night. It will not happen again."

Jacks stepped up to the case, peered in, then squared up within inches of Olgens. "Don't believe I ever seen a nigger second before."

Olgens stayed his ground. "We are here, sir, to accompany the gentlemen at hand. If you take issue with my being here, then you will take it up with Mr. Creed and Mr. Brody."

Wearing a smug look on his face, Brody nodded to Jacks to back off and said, "No matter who wins today, Edward, you will see the good Mr. Olgens Pierre in jail by sundown, or worse, for the murder of our dear, departed Baumgartner."

Olgens reached into the case, pulled out both knives, and held them up to Brody.

"A knife? You call these knives?" Brody asked and started laughing.

I made no acknowledgment to Brody, Jacks, or Olgens.

"Do you choose one of the two? Or . . . can I offer you this one?" Olgens held both knives by the blades in one hand while he elegantly waved the other hand over Frenchy's knife lying in the case.

Brody flinched, then pointed at mine. Olgens offered it to Jacks who then gingerly passed it on. Brody held it in his right hand, flipped it twice and over to his left, then back to his right. He nodded to Jacks.

Olgens gave to me my brother's knife. I was already intimately familiar with its weight and cut. I ran my finger across the blade, drawing a little blood. I caught Brody's eye and wiped the blood off with my thumb, then licked it. I nodded to my second with acceptance.

"Both have chosen their weapons," Olgens pronounced to our invited guests and a smattering of morning onlookers. "I ask but one question of the duelists. Will the gentle-men be tethered or untethered?"

I nodded again, not expecting my op-ponent to agree.

"Tethered," Brody said, with only a breath of hesitation.

"Tethered it is then, sirs."

Olgens drew out of the case a thin strip of leather about six feet long. He gestured that we shake left hands. Brody's hand was soft, like a man who had done little real work throughout his life. Jacks tied Brody's wrist while Olgens tied mine with only a two-foot length of leather swaying between us.

With the formalities complete, and one hand each bound together, we began to fight.

I gathered the slack of the tether and yanked tight, pulling Brody into me. Step-ping aside and from behind, I reached around to his right and sliced him lightly across the chest. He took a blind swipe and sliced my left thigh, cutting through the deerhide and drawing blood. I pushed away, spinning him back into a fighting stance. Not once did I take my eyes off of him.

"You come here to my home insulting me, I will kill you now," Brody said matter-of-factly.

"Feel your chest, sir. If I wanted, you'd be dead."

He touched his shirt with his knife hand and pulled it away to see blood. A slight frown crossed his face. I knew Brody was afraid. Bound together like this, I could almost feel his heart pounding through the leather.

We walked slowly in a circle. My thigh ached and I felt blood seeping from the wound. I heard nothing from our two parties as they stood under the oak trees on either side of the fighting ground. There was no cheering, only the silence of the early morning and our feet brushing through the grass.

Brody lunged at my left arm and shoulder. Still holding the leather bindings taut, I spun to my right and sliced his left forearm. As he glanced at his new wound, I yanked hard, pulling him off balance. I fell backward onto the grass and with my feet in his gut, flipped him over me. He slammed to the ground. I yanked once more, hard, wrenching his arm out of its socket. He tried to scream but could not. As he lay gasping for breath, I rolled to my knees and, still pulling on his arm, held my brother's knife to his throat. He tried to slice me again but I pinned his other arm down with my knee. The knife in his hand, my knife, dropped to the ground. I picked it up and with my left hand, cut the bindings that held us together. I tossed the knife to Olgens.

Jacks stepped in front of me and raised a pistol. From behind, I heard a sizzle and shot. Jacks flew backward to the ground with a hole the size of a silver dollar exploded in his chest. I twisted around to catch Billy lower his smoking pistol.

I still held Brody down with my knee. I did not know if he saw Billy shoot Jacks for he lay very still with a dazed look on his face. I softly whispered, "This ain't your home, ya goddamn Brit . . ."

As he cried out, I cut an exact circle on top of his head, grabbed a handful of hair, and with a pop, pulled his scalp off.

I sang in praise to *Watonga* and danced circles around Brody and Jacks. Seconds seemed like hours. I did not hear the gasps and cries of neither parties nor bystanders. In my mind, the world became a righteous blur of green trees, grass, and blood. I placed the fresh scalp on my belt with the others and began to walk away.

Sophie and Olgens stood over Brody's wreathing body. "You did not kill him?" I turned back to face them both. Rage contorted Sophie's face into that of a devil.

"You were supposed to *kill him*!" She screamed and snatched Frenchy's knife from Olgens's belt. She lunged toward Brody with the blade raised above her head. "You *will* die today, you bastard!"

Brody's wife suddenly dropped to her knees and leaned over her husband. Sophie blindly stabbed, burying the blade deep into her left shoulder. Olgens grabbed his sister before she could swing down again and wrenched the bloody knife away, dropping it to the grass.

"They would hang you for his murder," he whispered, dragging her away.

There was not much the physician could do for Brody except wrap a bandage around his head. I was fairly certain he would live. For his wife, it seemed much worse. She lay quiet next to her husband, shivering, her teeth chattering. The physician gently turned her and stuffed a piece of cloth into the cut. In an instant, the cloth was soaked with blood. The next piece also became soaked. He placed his right palm over the wound but could not stop her bleeding. Olgens still held Sophie tight some distance away from the scene, the only ones standing over the woman and the doctor were Juliette and I. Billy leaned against one of the oaks, watching us all.

"She's goin' to die by his hand," Juliette stated clearly. She reached down and with her fingers, dug up a handful of dirt and grass. She glanced to the physician, then to me, and shook her head.

I poked the doctor. "Juliette's right, by your hand she's gonna bleed to death, you need to get out of the way." He did not move. I pulled my knife, grabbed his hair, and pointed the blade at Brody. "Do ya wanna end like him?"

As soon as he stood, Juliette knelt down and filled the wound with the dirt and grass. I reached in and held my hand over hers as we both pressed against Mrs. Brody's shoulder. The bleeding slowed. I caught Juliette's eye. "He ain't no doctor," I said and gave her a wink. She gave me back a smile.

Brody began moaning and thrashing his arms. He reached around, pulled the bandage off, and tried touching what was left of the crown of his head. He screamed as his fingers pushed into the exposed mush that lay between skin and skull. His eyes rolled wild.

Sophie had gone limp in Olgens's arms. He gently stroked her hair. As I walked past them, they both stared at me without a word.

"Hey mate, where you going?" Billy hollered.

I kept walking. Where to, I did not know.

"Hey mate," Billy caught up with me. "Helluva a bloody morning, ay? How 'bout a drink?" He paused. "Uh, Zeb, you be cut pretty goddamn bad on your leg, mate."

"You're mighty happy, ain't ya?" I said. "For me just scalpin' your brother."

From behind me, Olgens shouted, "Mr. Creed, we have unfinished business, sir."

I shrugged them both off, for I wanted to feel nothing but the glory of the morning.

CHAPTER 28

The cut on my thigh was bleeding again, enough to soak through the sewed-up buckskin. I lay next to Billy in a wagon, flat on our backs, covered by burlap bags. All I smelled was the sickly sweet rot of the sugar beets they once held. The short road between New Orleans and Broussard's plantation was not smooth but filled with wagon ruts, so every jolt we took, a shooting pain increased to include the whole of my left leg. Benjamin Brody did not know how good he cut me.

"He was my uncle," Billy exclaimed, a little too loud.

"Who?" I whispered.

In the dead of night, I did not know if our words carried above the groans of the old wagon.

"Jacks, Uncle Eddy."

He took a long swig off the bottle he carried with him and nudged me with it. I took one long drink and handed it back. I thought for a second on how to respond. "Well, sir, I'm mighty grateful for you killin' your old Uncle Eddy. I wouldn't be lying here next to you under these God-awful bags of shit if it weren't for you killin' him. He wasn't no Brit, was he?"

Billy took a long breath and exhaled. "I hated the goddamn son-of-a-bitch."

"The night I killed Baumgartner, you stood out on Sophie's front porch with Brody and your uncle. Hell, I wanted to kill you."

"I understand, mate, and a worthy reason in your mind with all that you knew. However . . ." I felt his breath on me as he turned his head. He lowered his voice to a whisper. "By you knowing the true nature of things, way upriver, you would never have followed and would have been lost."

"Why?"

"Why would you have been lost? I thought it obvious. You couldn't find your way through St. Louis to Frenchy's without me."

"No, no. Why me? Why lead me down here to kill your brother?"

"Sophie wanted him dead. Frankly, I'm glad you left him living. Though I still don't understand the fascination with cutting another man's hair off."

287

I thought it odd that he did not flinch as Rudy lost his head, yet he found issue with the taking of a scalp. "Your brother, wherever he goes in this world, he'll suffer from losin' the top of his head. An' I will always be the man in this world who wears his scalp at my waist."

"As it should be, I suppose." Billy sighed.

"You didn't answer my question, why me?"

"Right time, right place. We knew about you not long after you punched ole Fitzpatrick's glasses up on Green River and decided to break from the fur company. So happens, you got caught in Baumgartner's snare. When him and Rudy came through St. Louis, taking yours and the other furs on down the river, word got out of two brothers. One shot dead with one left dying somewhere near Arrow Rock. Curious I was, so I left St. Louis and went to see if it might be you and still alive. The night I sat drinking with the good doctor I knew . . . you were the one. The one Sophie kept talking about, was going to make things right."

I lay in the jostling wagon, thinking back, trying to find a reason why I might be so special, so important that Billy would assist me in my journey to kill two men. I felt a burning, deep, as if somehow I had been used beyond my will. Though that made no sense, for it was I more than anyone else who wanted Rudy and Baumgartner dead.

"I still don't understand."

"Do you remember a night, two years ago, when you and your brother were last in New Orleans? On the porch of Sophie's house, you stopped a man from entering?"

I closed my eyes. "I remember stoppin' a man who openly held a pistol. It was late and I needed fresh air. He came up the steps. He didn't see me in the shadows. I knew Sophie was inside and when he flung the door open an' pointed the pistol straight at her . . . well, I had to do somethin'."

"You saved her from assassination."

After I hit him with the butt end of my knife, he went down. There came such a commotion and he was carted off. I did not see his face it was covered in so much blood. Jonathan and I left New Orleans the next morning, early. I never knew the outcome of the man, nor the reason why he was to shoot Sophie right there in her own parlor.

For a few long seconds, only the squeak of the wagon wheels could be heard. Billy whispered, "A strong impression you made on her, mate, she never forgot. When your name came a floating down the river along

289

with word of your escapades at Rendezvous, a message was sent to fetch you, so to speak . . . But, as I have already mentioned, Baumgartner snared you and things went awry. It then became my duty to help you seek your revenge."

"Why?"

Even in the back of a rolling wagon, hidden under stinking burlap bags, I felt him tense up at my simple question. He took another long drink. Then, "As I said, mate, for reasons that go back many years, I hated that son-of-a-bitch uncle of mine, and Baumgartner . . . as much as you." He spat the words out as if they were poison on his tongue. "I hate my brother even more."

I remembered the evening at the opera, Billy always standing a little behind, Brody's sharp words and demanding him light his cigar. The utter disrespect Brody and Jacks showed in public to their own flesh and blood.

We lay in silence for a while. If I were to die that night, I wanted the whole story. "Frenchy?" I asked in a loud voice.

From the driver's side of the buckboard, Olgens rustled the bags. "Shhh now, if we're found out, they'll kill us 'fore we get there!" The wagon kept clattering forward.

There came a long pause. Then, in a

whisper, Billy continued, as if he recited his words from a book. "Knew him, growing up in Barataria and New Orleans. Used to help him sometimes find . . . women of a certain color. He was particularly fond of quadroons, if you know what I mean. It's how he and Sophie met. He was a bloody powerful man and could have any woman but she placed her spell on him, keeping him from all the others. She had another man in secret. He and Frenchy were partners in certain business deals in New Orleans. When the baby came, she decided who she wanted and sent Benjamin to kill Frenchy. As you found, my brother is not the most courageous of men. Frenchy's heart was not cut out but was broken and shamed. He disappeared into the swamps of Terre Bonne with the baby, never to be seen in Louisiana again, leaving his kingdom in the hands of his own brothers. All that he built, all that he plundered, slipped into debauchery and decay."

The wagon was slowing. Our time of talk was almost done.

"But what of Sophie?"

"She could never spell me like she's done you and all the others. So we have an understanding."

"Like me an' the others," I whispered to

myself. "And Frenchy?"

"Especially Frenchy. Even more so does the daughter have her spell on him."

Asking no more questions, I lay there, still feeling burned. Even more burned by hearing Billy speak what sounded like the truth.

"I'm glad you took his scalp and left him alive. He deserves it," Billy said slowly, as if he savored every word.

The wagon stopped. Within seconds, the silence of the swamp surrounding us was deafening.

Olgens lifted one of the burlap bags and shined the oil lamp on us. "Shhh now, I tell you, we are almost to the gate. You must be ready for anything." He stopped and jerked his head away, as if he heard something. "Dawn is approaching," he said in a low voice and covered us back up.

The wagon lurched forward.

Billy cleared his throat. "Margo will be with the unmarried women and her boys will be with the men. Their names are Abe and Sturgis, Abe being the oldest. All three know me, but you . . ." He felt for my hand and pressed a coin into its palm. "This will secure their trust."

Holding the coin for a few seconds, I rubbed the two faces with my thumb and forefinger, wondering which side was the back, which might be the front. I placed it in my belt and sighed.

"When all here is done," Billy whispered, "you and me, mate, we're sailing to Texas. Volunteers are gathering now in New Orleans. I hear they give away the bloody land." He sounded excited. "Though we might have to kill a few Mexicans once we get there."

I said nothing, as I had not considered any possible future to come.

The wagon's wheels ground to a stop. Olgens shook the top bag and sat quiet. I heard footsteps and heavy breathing.

"You there, boy. Where you come from an' who's yer master?"

"Come from Laura, sir. Master's name's Higgins, sir."

Through the cloth of the bags, I could see the shadow of a torch as the man lifted it up to get a better glimpse of Olgens. I held my breath.

"Don't see no badge, boy. Master Higgins let his niggas roam free?" The man took a shallow breath and chuckled.

"No, sir!" Olgens paused and fumbled through his pockets. I felt Billy tense up. I held my knife in one hand and with the other, ready to throw the bags aside. I heard a piece of paper being unfolded.

"Yes, sir, I got this here from the proprietor an' he say should be good 'nough."

There was more shallow breathing then the rustle of paper as the man handled it not two feet from my head. "Ain't got no badge, just a piece a old paper." More breathing. "What you sent here to do, boy?"

"Sir, Master Higgins say he sent word on ahead to ya'll . . . I's to collect yall's cane cuts an' put 'em in these here bags an' deliver 'em on back to the proprietor at Laura . . . an' Master Higgins say get a receipt else he beat ole Olgens good now."

"Olgens yer name?"

"Yes, sir, Olgens be my name."

From somewhere beyond the road, I could hear the earliest egrets began to stir, their caws echoing through the cyprus trees.

"Hum, ain't never heard a nigga called Olgens before."

"No, expect you haven't . . . sir."

The man walked slowly around to the back of the wagon, dragging the wood handle of the torch along the shallow sideboard, and stopped. With the fire raised above his head, I could see his large upper-half in silhouette. "All these here bags empty?" He switched the torch to his left hand and fumbled with one of the back latches. The wagon began inching backward.

"Ho boy, hold them mules!" He hollered, then silence.

"Only thing sitting in them bags is the smell a' rotten beets, sir."

The man stood for a second or two more, then dragged the torch along the passenger side and heaved himself up to sit next to Olgens.

"Let's go, boy, ain't got all day."

Olgens released the break and with his reins, strapped the two mules on down the road. Within ten or so minutes, we stopped. Both Olgens and the man climbed down off the wagon and without a word to each other, walked away.

All was quiet except for a dog barking in the distance. I eased one of the bags off me and peered over the top of the wagon rail into the dark opening of a barn. There was no light to see by but for a half-moon and the morning stars. Earlier, at Sophie's, Billy told of him and Frenchy visiting the plantation many years before, and how he knew his way around. I trusted him that nothing had changed. He pushed aside the bags, climbed over the sideboard, and with the creak of the wagons' struts, let himself down to the ground. With my leg stiffened up, I followed, making as little noise as I could. I eased over the sideboard and Billy helped me to the ground. The pain in my thigh was searing. I felt the stitches might burst.

"You all right, mate?" Billy whispered.

With my head lowered, I forced myself to stand alone, my weight and hand pressed upon the wound. I wiped blood on my smock, looked up, and nodded with a shrug.

I would not let him know how bad I hurt.

A little past the barn lay what must have been the livery stable and the bar gate of a corral. The random whinnies of workhorses could be heard as we passed. A couple of pigs snorted from somewhere behind the building. The crow of the rooster would soon follow. Broussard's plantation was awakening.

Billy motioned to follow him to a row of shacks built identical to the other. Beyond, near an acre of open field was bathed in the waning moonlight. In the distance, shrouded in darkness and mist, lay the great swamp of Terre Bonne.

We stopped at the first shack. "If I remember right, the boys will be in one of the first three," Billy whispered. "As I said, mate, their names are Abe and Sturgis. Tell them to leave all belongings behind. I will find their mother. Be quick, we must meet back here before dawn's light." He faced me and stuck out his hand. For a second, he stood smiling. I reached out and we shook. As I let go, he was gone.

I stood in the shadows for a long while, fumbling with the coin he had given to me. Though there was a chill in the air, I wiped beads of sweat from my forehead. I bent my left knee back and forth a couple of times and massaged my thigh, again wiping blood on my smock. I felt the pain but was not so stiff that I could not fight or run if need be. I looked up to the last of the evening stars. *"Well, Zeb,"* I whispered to myself. *"At least it ain't rainin'."*

From the wagon, I heard the overseer muttering. I could not understand what he was saying, but by the tone of his voice, he seemed to have become impatient with Olgens. I heard the wagon creak forward and then stop. He said, "Boy, I told ya we goin' this a way!"

"Yes, sir, yes, sir!" Olgens replied and he loudly switched the mules into action.

I crept onto the porch and entered the shack. Even in total darkness, I sensed the many sleeping bodies. The room smelled of ancient soil and sweat, of men who may have never bathed in their lives. My head spun as I recognized this smell. For an instant, I was back tied to a stake with my brother, like dogs, behind my father's teepee. I bumped the first bed and a man groaned. I leaned down and whispered, "Lookin' fer two boys, brothers, Abe an' Sturgis."

With my eyes grown accustomed to the dark, I could see the silhouette of the man's head and his white eyes. He sat up and stared closely at my face. "Does I know ya, sir?"

"No. I'm lookin' for the boys, can ya help?" I whispered.

Some of the other men began to stir. I whispered again, with more urgency. "Can you help?"

The man slowly nodded. "They be in the next house over."

I was confused. "The house closest to this one or the one past that?"

"The next house over, sir," he repeated.

The groans from the other men became words, most I did not know. I left out the front door.

Entering the second shack, there seemed to be fewer men, the lay of the beds were different and there was an oil lamp lit, very low. As I was about to shake the first man, someone near the rear wall picked up the lamp, lit it bright, and began speaking. I snaked my way through the sleeping men to stand in front of him. "Do you know two brothers, Abe an' Sturgis?"

Not responding to my direct question, he said loudly, "Master don't know stranger! Master be pissed." He saw the blood on my britches, began to swing the lamp in an arc and to speak in gibberish. I asked again, trying to catch his attention. His voice grew louder. "Master don't know stranger! Master don't know stranger! Master don't know shit 'bout no stranger!"

Everyone in the house was now sitting upright in their beds, staring at me. I walked right through them, back to the door, and announced, "Two brothers, Abe an' Sturgis. I'm here to help 'em." My hand shook as I pulled the coin from my belt and held it up to the swinging light for all to see. With the commotion, I was near a panic to find those boys and get away.

A young man of maybe fifteen stood and with an astonished look on his face said, "I'm Abe, sir." A boy a year or two younger stood up next to him. In their chocolate skin and high cheekbones, I saw both Olgens and Sophie. For an instant, I saw Jonathan and me.

"The coin, sir? Where did you get the coin?" the young man asked.

"I'm here to take you away!" I responded and went to usher them out the door.

Louder the crazy man spoke and moved swiftly toward the door, as if to cut us off. Some of the other men were standing.

The younger boy was in tears. "Papa. That be Papa's gold doubloon, Abe."

The older brother also wiped tears from his eyes. "Sir, the only one who might have that coin would be Uncle Olgens." He stopped. "Mama?"

I stepped toward him and offered the coin. "Billy's gettin' your Mama right now. We must go, else we're all dead!"

"Master don't know stranger!" The man reached over and attempted to slap the coin from my hand. I was too quick.

"Georgy!" Someone hollered from the shadows. He stopped his gibberish and turned toward the voice. From behind, Abe swung a water jug and struck him hard in the back of the head. The lamp slipped from his hand and spilled to the floor. In an instant, oil and flames washed across the wood planks, lighting rags of bedrolls on fire. Every man and boy pushed to get out. I stepped onto the porch and to the side of the door. Next to me, smoke poured out the top of the only window. I did not see Georgy escape. I fell to my knees and peered back into the burning building. Inside the door, beneath thick smoke,

Georgy laid unconscious, bleeding and trampled on. I reached in, grabbed both his wrists and dragged him out to the common yard. By then, the shack was engulfed.

The screams of fire sounded through all the slave quarters. The yard filled with the resident men, women, and crying children. One by one, their homes went up in flames. They did nothing to quench the fires.

Billy was beside me. "We must go, *now!*" he shouted and pointed the way across the field to the swamp. He herded the mother and her two sons to run across the deep ruts furrowed through the soil. I followed with my pistols pulled, limping from my wound. Our steps were not swift and from behind us, there rose such chaos the whole parish must have heard. As dawn spread its light on us, warning bells began to ring. Still hobbling, I glanced back over my shoulder to see if anyone followed. I lost my balance and fell. I tried to stand, but could not. Blood had soaked through the whole left side of my britches. As Billy reached the edge of the field, he gave a high-pitched whistle. Within seconds, Sophie's two boatmen appeared and gathered the newly freed family together. I could only watch as they disappeared down into the darkness of the swamp.

Billy stood for a second, looking past me, then turned and started toward where the family had been. I lowered my head and again tried to stand. I heard boots in the dirt and flipped over to lie in a rut, on my back with my pistols pointed and cocked. I shut my eyes for a second and with the back of my blood-streaked hand, wiped the dirt and sweat off my brow. I opened them and Billy leaned in, smiled, and said, "Not a bad rescue, aye mate?"

I closed my eyes again and breathed a heavy sigh.

"Aye, mate," I said and looked up at him. "Not bad for a goddamn Brit."

He pulled me to my feet and dragged me to the swamp. Beyond the field there dropped a steep slope of maybe fifteen feet to the water's shore. Margo and her sons sat in the same shallow boat Sophie had arrived in at Pawpaw's only a few nights before. They waved at us to hurry. Billy eased me to the ground. With a hand on my shoulder, he gently pushed. I began to slowly slide down slick vines and dead leaves. From across the field echoed a *sha-boom*. Billy's hand jerked away. I looked up to see him pitch at a most unnatural position, as if his whole back had been cracked. He touched the blood soaking through his shirt and stared at me in stunned surprise. I tried to stop from sliding, to make my way back up to him. A second *sha-boom* came an instant later and he was blown off his feet and sent reeling down on top of me. We both splashed face first into the black water.

I lay still, in silence, with Billy's lifeless body sinking me deep into the mud. I felt that I could breathe if I only opened my mouth. Breathe in the whole swamp, as I once saw Olgens do. I knew I was not to die that day. I knew in my soul I would live on and remember the weight that pressed upon me.

Hands reached down, pulled me up, and placed me in the boat.

"Where's Billy?" I asked.

No one spoke.

I started to slip over the side. One of the boatmen stopped me. The two brothers jumped into the water and raised Billy's body up from the mud. We made room for him.

Silently, we slipped south, disappearing into the morning mist of the Terre Bonne.

CHAPTER 29

On a funeral pyre made of old bones, cut cypress, oak, and wrapped in Spanish moss, we burned Billy's body at sunset, next to Pawpaw's home on the water, near where the gator had hung. Smoke and cinders billowed up to the stars. Standing alone at the edge of the clearing, I saw fireflies dance away through the trees and disappear.

I sang him a Lakota death song. It was much later that I wept for him.

Olgens came the next morning saying that with the fire and all the commotion, he drove that old wagon straight out the plantation's gates and all the way back to New Orleans. His reunion with Margo and her boys was indeed joyous. That evening, we feasted on roasted gator, bluegill, greens, and the roots of cattails. The mood was bittersweet, as we all knew the life it took to free them.

Olgens led us in a prayer. "Lord, have

mercy on Billy's soul. A good man he was, a righteous man. Never hurt no one. And if he did, didn't mean to." He glanced at me. "Retribution is not ours to receive, but the Lord's to give. In our Christ's name . . ."

Everyone followed with amen.

Olgens, Pawpaw, and I sat on the porch and smoked. The silence between us felt comfortable, like we were old friends.

I did not know what to do or where to go. I said as much to them.

"You must come with us to Haiti. I'll insure you live very comfortably, my friend," Olgens kindly offered.

I said thanks and gave him as gracious a look as I could muster.

Pawpaw proposed I stay with him in his home, saying I could hunt, fish, catch *gatas* for the rest of my days and be happy. Again, with a sense of gratitude, I shook my head no.

"Might head back up to Missouri . . ." I suggested. "See some friends near Arrow Rock."

Olgens sheepishly smiled. I did not remember ever telling him of the doctor and his daughter. I smiled also, though more to myself than to him.

"Might strike out west, back to the Rockies. Though I hear there ain't many beaver left to trap," I said with only half a heart.

Then, out of the blue, I announced, "Hell, I think I'll go to Texas. I hear they're givin' away the bloody land!" I was shocked to hear Billy's voice echo in my own. "Of course, I might have to kill a few Mexicans while I'm there." I slapped my thigh in excitement and winced in pain. All three of us busted up laughing.

"That certainly would be a prudent thing for you to do, Mr. Creed," Olgens stated. Pawpaw nodded in agreement.

We sat smoking for a while longer. Olgens and his grandfather retired for the evening, joining Margo and the boys in the warm, crowded house. I stayed outside, alone, enjoying the cool air. I slept without dreaming.

Olgens left the next morning with his brother's wife and sons, headed south to the Isle of Grande Terre to catch a small schooner and on to Haiti. I wished them all well.

I doubted I would ever see Olgens Pierre again.

Before leaving, Abe and Sturgis gave to me their father's coin I had given them the morning of the rescue. Again, I rubbed the two faces with my thumb and forefinger. There was no difference.

That night, Pawpaw and I sat out under a sky full of brilliant, shining stars. I realized it had not rained in several days. I mentioned this to the old man.

"Only time it's rain, is when ya feel it hit yer face. All the other time, it water pourin' from the sky," he proudly exclaimed and laughed.

I smiled and we returned back to the quiet of the evening. Nothing more was needed to be said.

ABOUT THE AUTHOR

Originally from Oklahoma, **Mark C. Jackson** is an accomplished songwriter, performer, and poet who currently resides near San Diego, California, with his lovely wife Judy, their dog Brody, and cat Brook. This is his first novel.